Haverstraw

Haverstraw

By

Margaret Williams

AVOCET PRESS INC

Published by
Avocet Press Inc
19 Paul Court
Pearl River, NY 10965
http://www.avocetpress.com
books@avocetpress.com

AVOCET PRESS

Library of Congress Cataloging-in-Publication Data
Williams, Margaret, 1930 Feb. 15-
Haverstraw / by Margaret Williams.
p. cm.
ISBN 0-9725078-1-7 (alk. paper)
1. Haverstraw (N.Y.)—Fiction. 2. Irish Americans—Fiction. 3.
Married people—Fiction. 4. Brickworks—Fiction. I. Title.
PS3623.I5586H38 2004
813'.6—dc22
2003015836

Printed in the USA
First Edition

For Earl

1

Overhead St. Leo's great iron bell pealed out the good news of Easter, joined by the distant bells of churches scattered throughout the Hudson River Valley. Remnants of the congregation, dressed in their Sunday best, lingered after Mass to exchange greetings, share gossip, and delay returning to the isolation of their farms. Nineteen-hundred-and-four marked Anne Beauvois's first spring in Chestnut Grove. She stood at the foot of the church steps with Yvette LeFleur and Helene Gaudet. Whenever their conversation was drowned by the clamor of the bell, they'd break into giggles of delight. Anne was reminded of how intensely she missed the company of women.

Bright yellow forsythia, forced into early bloom by the women of the Altar Society, had filled their church with captive sunlight as the voices of the choir had filled it with alleluias. The dreary weeks of Lent had ended. Soon there would be soft warm breezes and the rich smell of earth after rain. And soon she could leave her mother's heavy cloak on the hook behind the cabin door, free at last of the weight of winter.

Anne saw her father free Willow's reins from the hitching rail along the cemetery wall, the cemetery where, last October, she had watched her mother's coffin disappear beneath soil and rocks. Next month, she would bring a jar of water and sow flower seeds on the grave. Her father might not mind waiting the little time it would take to do that.

Anne hurriedly said goodbye to Helene and Yvette, gathered her long skirts, and moved quickly toward her father, calling out, "I'm coming, Father."

Anticipating his help up into the wagon, for she was wearing one of her best dresses, she was dismayed to find him already seated, his back stiffly arched, his face stony. Bewildered, she braced her foot on a spoke of the front wheel, and, with effort, hoisted herself up into the wagon, praying that the splintery wood not catch and tear her gown. Embarrassed and chagrined that Helene and Yvette and the rest of the congregation had witnessed her father's lack of manners, Anne's face burned and her heart began to race. She wondered what had set him off this time.

Beneath a gray chinchilla jacket, with matching hat and muff — Uncle Henri's graduation gift — she wore one of three silk gowns she'd brought with her last October from Quebec, having had no idea of how unsuitable such gowns would be for Chestnut Grove. Helene and Yvette, with perhaps a slight trace of envy, had complimented her profusely on her outfit. The dress was a plaid, bright green and white, with rows of ruffles at the hem. It had lain in her trunk, carefully folded by Celeste, her aunt's maid, who'd helped them hurriedly pack for the frantic train ride from Canada.

Six months had passed since her mother died. Yesterday, Anne decided it was time to put away the dark clothing. A pretty dress for Easter would relieve the tedium of her father's farm.

Anne had barely taken her place on the wagon when her father lashed the whip against Willow's haunch. The startled animal lurched forward, jerking the wagon and causing Anne to clutch the edge of her seat with her left hand, her right hand imprisoned in the muff. The iron-rimmed wheels clattered noisily over the hard red clay of Chestnut Grove's country roads as her father continued to flog the beast and Willow strained to outrun the leather.

Anne promised herself that later, after her father had lit his pipe and was settled into his chair beside the fire for his Sunday nap, she would slip into the barn, and stroke Willow's neck to console him. And tell him that he was a good horse, a fine horse, and that her father was mean and cruel.

Her concern for the horse was interrupted by her father, muttering ugly French oaths, sounds that had terrified her when she was a child. He spoke only his native French, although he understood English quite well. He shared the Québecois creed of *la survivance* with many others who left farms behind in Canada. Drummed into them at weekly Mass in Biddeford by the curé, to save them from the evils of assimilation. Despite fourteen years in Maine, and another four here in New York, her father claimed that someday he would return to Quebec.

As the wagon flew and the wheels crashed over the half-frozen ground, Anne stifled an instinct to cry out a warning; it would only provoke her father further. Furious, incomplete phrases spilled from his mouth.

Anne quickly reviewed the events of the day. Earlier, before they left for church, had his eyes narrowed when he first helped her up into the wagon? Perhaps he was offended because she no longer wore her mother's black cloak. Or perhaps Mr. Lessard had spoken to him?

While he had not struck her for many years, not since long before she left to study in Quebec, Anne still remembered the sting of his palm on her cheek, the searing burn of his belt around her calf. She clutched the wooden seat and murmured, "Blessed Lady, Blessed Mother," over and over until, at last, the peaked roof of her father's barn appeared and Willow turned up the familiar lane.

Her father jerked hard on the reins, and the wagon slowed to a halt outside the barn. Anne alighted quickly from the wagon, holding her skirts away from the rough wood. Still, a splinter caught a hem and she heard the fabric rip. Intent on escaping her father, she hurried into the cabin to change her clothes and begin breakfast. The smell of biscuits and fried ham might distract him.

Her father quickly followed behind her to the doorway of the cabin, his voice filled with loathing. "Such fine clothes — such a lady." As she feared, she had disrespected her mother's memory by wearing her green plaid dress.

"Too fine for a good man like Lucien Lessard. Too fine — to marry a farmer."

Ah, not the dress. Instead, Mr. Lessard.

While she had been speaking with Helene and Yvette, her father must have encountered Lucien Lessard and probably grasped his neighbor's hand heartily, confident that the marriage business was settled. Confident he would soon have a son-in-law to help with plowing and planting. Only to learn that was not to happen.

Terrified by the growing intensity of her father's rage, she quickly looked around, saw a knife lying alongside the stone sink, and slipped backward until she was near it.

Anne clearly remembered nights back in Maine, when her father, dissatisfied, would fling his supper plate across the table, or against the kitchen wall. She fumbled behind her, until her fingers closed around the handle of the knife. Would she have the courage to use it?

Anne had sent a letter to Lucien Lessard declining his kind and generous offer of marriage. She had no intention of marrying a forty-year old widower with six daughters, an old man with green teeth. She did not tell Mr. Lessard that she had a life to return to up in Canada. By the time the summer was over, her trunk would be packed and she'd be on her way back to *rue Ste. Geneviève*, back to Aunt Josie and Uncle Henri.

She would leave as soon as she'd found someone to keep house for her father. Unfortunately, it was during her attempts to do this that the trouble began with Mr. Lessard. She'd paid him a visit to inquire if his oldest daughter, Marie, might be willing to cook and clean in exchange for eggs or milk. Instead, Mr. Lessard decided he needed Anne to care for his own family.

Her father's face was twisted with rage as he shook a clenched fist at her. "You! You're old! Your looks are gone…finished. You're skinny. A real bean pole. Lessard doesn't care — he already had a pretty wife. He would have overlooked that you were a teacher, for the sake of his family.

"And…," his voice began to squeal, "… to write to him. To send a letter, knowing, all the time knowing that someone else would have to read it to him…." He shook his head repeatedly. This insult was beyond belief.

Her father's squat body blocked the way out of the cabin. Anne's single thought was to escape. If she climbed the ladder to the loft where she slept, he might follow her. Her fingers tightened around the handle of the the knife, then released it.. Even if he hit her, she could not strike back. He was her father. Her insides twisting with pain, she tucked her arms across her chest and bent her shoulders forward to ward off his words, but did not lower her eyes.

"Worthless! That's what you are…useless! You can't even milk a cow. A fine, fine lady in your fancy dress."

Both his hands, now clenched into fists, were pressed against his stomach. He held them there, and then dropped them, palms open and limp against the trousers of his Sunday suit. With slumped shoulders he turned and left the cabin.

Anne watched carefully from the window above the sink as her father reached for Willow's bridle and began to lead the animal toward the barn. She dashed across the slate floor and out of the cabin, across the pasture and down to a glen where she had hidden in the past, concealed by a stand of tall hemlocks. She lifted the hem of her long skirts as she scrambled down the rocky hillside, briefly lost her balance, tumbled against a tree trunk and felt a tug on her sleeve. Her dress was torn, ruined.

When she reached the glen and was out of sight of her father's barn, she paused, her face in her hands. She began to sob.

"Blessed Mother, help me. Dear St. Anne, please, help me," she gasped.

Worthless…? After she had given up her perfect life in Canada to take care of him.

Useless…? She had cooked his food, boiled his filthy trousers, dragged the manure-crusted fabric across an iron washboard and scrubbed it with a brush until her hands were red and chapped, her knuckles scarred, her fingernails ragged. She had left behind in Canada everything she cared about for this horrid existence.

After the funeral, Aunt Josie had taken her aside and told her she should stay with her father.

"He's alone, now, Anne and he needs you. For a little while. Then you will come back to us."

At first, Anne pretended her mother was away visiting some distant place. When she finally was able to admit that her mother was gone, a hollowness grew inside her.

When she had first left Maine, Anne had ached for her mother and wrote to her every night. But life with Aunt Josie and Uncle Henri was pleasant. Her schoolwork kept her busy and there was less time left for letter writing. Anne wished now she had written more frequently. Why had she not saved even one of her mother's letters?

Over the five years in Quebec, her aunt became her mother. Anne came to depend on Aunt Josie for advice. This sophisticated woman knew the answer to everything. She showed Anne how to gracefully reach down and gather her gown at the knee and lift it slightly when ascending a staircase. Taught her how to twist her long auburn curls and fasten them behind her head with tortoiseshell combs. Only once had Anne not sought her aunt's counsel. Aunt Josie would never have approved of Paul.

Reluctantly, Anne had agreed to remain at Chestnut Grove, but only until she could find a hired girl to take over the cooking and cleaning. Then she would be released to take the train back to Canada and resume teaching. Her weekends would be spent on *rue Ste. Geneviève*, in her own cozy room with the feather bed and the window seat that looked out across the park. Anne would find Paul and explain why she had never returned to the bookstore.

A scratching sound in the leaves that covered the floor of the glen startled her. A gray squirrel darted into the clearing where Anne was seated on a fallen log. It froze at the sight of her, then scrambled up a tree trunk and hid in the crotch of a high branch, curled into a ball, still as a statue.

She had to admit that part of what her father said was true. She could not even help with the cows. Her terror of the huge, dull beasts made her clumsy and she'd overturned the milk pail so often, that he no longer allowed her near the barn.

But old? Was she really old? At twenty-three? And no longer attractive? She had never been pretty, but she received compliments for her eyes and her curly hair. Paul said she was lovely, the loveliest woman he had ever seen.

Had it been one of her brothers who'd graduated school, become a teacher, perhaps her father might have bragged about it. Probably not. For him, farming was "God's work—the only fit work for a man." He had counted on his sons' help but, barely a month after they arrived at the farm in New York, her brothers declared a preference for the livelier streets of Biddeford, Maine, gathered their few clothes in a sack, and took off down the lane. Her mother wrote to Anne that her father had flung a pitchfork at their retreating backs and allowed it to lie where it had fallen for several days, while he sat by the fire rubbing his forehead. Despite her weakened heart, his wife joined him in the fields.

Anne had never considered that Lessard could not read. Now she recalled the shame her father had suffered, married to a woman who could read books, letters, and newspapers, and pass along to him important information she thought he might need. But Anne's mother had eventually stopped because of the desperation in her husband's eyes. He would look over at her each time he heard her turn a page. When her mother married Etienne Beauvois, she had understood that she would have to make sacrifices.

One evening shortly after her mother's funeral, the supper dishes washed and the cabin tidied, Anne had brought out her copy of *Pride and Prejudice* from her trunk and sat down at the long kitchen table. She had read only a few pages before her father, seated before the fireplace smoking his pipe, objected to her waste of oil. The next day she found some tallow candles, but the smell of rancid fat broke into the story. Anne placed the book back in her trunk.

Anne shook her head to clear her thoughts and wiped her tears on the torn sleeve of her dress. She might be different from the women of Chestnut Grove, but her father was wrong. She was not worthless.

As she climbed back to her father's cabin she decided she would no longer hide from her father or fear him. Her head erect, her shoulders thrust back, she smiled. She would leave this dreadful place. Her father's outburst had released her. So he considered her worthless? Good. She would now write to Aunt Josie that her father said he did not need her. Perhaps Anne might send a note to the bookstore.

She would speak to her father after he had eaten dinner. before he fell into his nap. She would keep her eyes on St. Anne, on the little statue her mother had kept on the kitchen shelf back in Biddeford, which now sat on the shelf above the fireplace.

As far as Anne knew, her mother stood up to her husband only once, the time she insisted that their daughter would not go to work in the cotton mill. Anne's life was not to be wasted amid bobbins and looms. Anne overheard her remind him how St. Anne had saved their child when she was very ill as an infant. Despite his strong objection, for he was counting on Anne's salary, she sent a letter to her sister, Josie, in Quebec City and the matter was settled. Anne would leave Maine to live with Josie and her husband, Henri, and attend the *Monastère des Ursulines*, the convent school on *rue Donnacona*, where Josie and Anne's mother had studied, and she would live the life her mother had abandoned when she married.

Anne strode purposefully across the cow pasture, holding her skirts above her ankles, avoiding the scattered piles of dung. She remembered the narrow cobblestone streets and horse-drawn *calèches* bearing ladies in elegantly feathered *chapeaux*. In the winter, sleighs skimmed over packed-down snow and, after the huge snow banks melted, grassy green parks were lined with blossoms of every color.

Her aunt and uncle's home was a small brownstone tucked behind the Chateau Frontenac, on *rue Ste. Geneviève*, more discretely impressive than the huge white clapboard houses with black shutters in Saco, across the river from Biddeford, where the wealthy families lived. Back when she was a child, she'd thought the houses in Saco were the finest in the world.

The Ursuline nuns had smiled when they learned she was Josie's niece. Each year more friends, more adventures. She was taught to speak proper Parisian French, to read and converse in English. Now and then an evening at the opera, or the ballet or, her favorite, the symphony. The dinners, the dances, the holiday balls. Traveling by train to Quebec on Friday and back again on Monday to Beaupré, where she taught school.

She thought about Paul halting the carriage in the grove of trees and kissing her.

The long table was cleared, the pots and dishes washed, and the leftover *cassoulet* covered and stored in the pantry. Her father was seated beside the fire, his head bent as he concentrated on dampening his pipe in preparation for his nap. Anne straightened the curtain above the sink, finding small tasks to postpone the confrontation with her father. She crossed the slate floor toward him. Impulsively, she reached out to the mantle for the statue of St. Anne, then clutched it against her breast.

"Papa," she began. The word came out as a whisper. "Papa!" she repeated, her voice clearer, more forceful. Her father raised his head slightly, his eyes closed. He had been silent during dinner, studiously ignoring her. Anne's insides churned. She held the statue more tightly.

"Papa, I am sorry you do not have sons here to help you, and, as you say, I am of no use to you. I am leaving. First I will find someone to cook for you; then I am returning to Quebec."

His eyes flew open. He raised his head further and gave her a guarded look.

"I have no money for trains to Quebec," he said warily.

"Aunt Josie gave me my return ticket before she left."

"Josie!" he grunted. "Josie." He closed his eyes, lowered his head, and said no more.

2

Anne's day centered around these midday hours, as she listened for the sound of the mail wagon. A month had already passed since she had written to Aunt Josie, with no reply. Each afternoon she stayed near the cabin door and, at the faintest sound of hooves or wheels, she left whatever chore she was doing and hurried outside to scan the road for the postman.

On a sunny day in mid-May a letter finally arrived, addressed in a strong masculine hand. From Paul? No, it was from Uncle Henri. A slip of paper fell out of the letter. When Anne picked it up she saw it was a check for three hundred dollars, made out to her. She sat down on the makeshift bench outside the cabin door, her heart racing.

After she'd read the first paragraph of her uncle's letter, she fell back against the rough wood and pressed her eyes shut. Darling Aunt Josie.

Her aunt had slipped on the ice as she'd hurried out of her house last February. She'd struck her head against the front stone steps and died. The house on *rue Ste. Geneviéve* was to be leased and he was moving to Toronto to live with his sister. He asked for her prayers.

There no longer was a home for her in Quebec.

The numbing grief which had crippled her following the death of her mother was stirred back to life. It clouded her mind and sapped her strength. She searched for someone with whom she could share her loneliness. Anne wrote her brothers about the accident and told her father.

"Good riddance," he grunted.

Anne resumed wearing the dark clothes she'd donned after her mother died.

Then Anne wrote to Louise. Six years before, when Anne had left Maine for Quebec, she had started a casual correspondence with Louise Fournier, whose family lived in the same tenement in Biddeford with Anne. Louise filled her letters with gossip of the neighborhood, the births and marriages and the doings at St. Andre's, where they had each received their sacraments. Louise's father started work at the Biddeford Textile Mill as a young boy and, eventually, was promoted to supervisor in the weaving room, where it was his job to monitor the thread the spinning bobbins fed into the clattering looms. Unfortunately, one day he reached into a loom to retie a broken thread and his sleeve was caught by a whirling belt. Instantly, his arm and then his hand was dragged into the maw of the machine. From her friend's letters, it was apparent that Louise's father had become a bitter recluse.

Anne had written to Louise last summer, confiding in her about Paul. About their visit to the falls in Montmorency, and the sunny afternoon when they joined the Sunday strollers who flocked to the promenade that overlooked the St. Lawrence River, the day when Paul told her she was lovelier than any other woman on the crowded boardwalk. She had described his thick brown hair and his soft gray eyes, and why he was not to be blamed for his divorce.

Louise's immediate reply was filled with grim reminders of the sixth and the tenth commandments, and Anne felt betrayed. She was foolish to have trusted Louise. She did not answer that letter. Then word came of her mother's grave illness and soon Anne found herself trapped in Chestnut Grove.

This time, however, Louise's reply was warm. She wrote that a memorial Mass had been celebrated for Anne's mother at St. Andre's when the news of her death last October had reached Biddeford. Her mother had been loved and highly respected.

The renewal of their friendship stirred in Anne the desire to see her old friend. After some thought, she sent an inquiry to the Mother Superior in Biddeford, asking for a teaching assignment at one of their schools. Her plan was to return to Biddeford where she would keep house for her brothers. She and Louise might take the train into Portland each weekend, maybe lunch at a little tea room. Or take an occasional trip to Boston where they could window shop along Tremont Street, visit the Museum of Fine Arts, or perhaps attend a concert at Symphony Hall.

It would be better than Chestnut Grove where she'd spent the past week picking apples, sorting them into baskets by size and quality, then dragging the baskets, which were too heavy to carry, to the wagon. It was the hardest work she had ever done. Her father grumbled that she was slow.

Mr. Lessard resumed his visits to their cabin. Lately he had started dropping by after supper, while Anne was still busy at the sink.

Lessard and her father sat beside the fire and smoked their pipes and shared memories of their boyhoods, while the dying flames slowly became embers. Anne knew the stories by heart, of a time free of hardship and struggle. On those evenings, Anne fled to the loft and drew the quilt over her head in a vain effort to smother their voices.

3

Anne dutifully accompanied her father to church every week, fulfilling her Sunday obligation, but at the end of Mass hurried back to the wagon, avoiding the intimacy of neighborly gossip. Until one Sunday in August when Yvette and Helene waylaid her, their arms outstretched.

They excitedly described a church dance down river in Haverstraw to which the whole congregation was invited.

Yvette implored her, "Annie, you cannot miss it. You must come. Haverstraw is magnificent. Every sort of shop, and the loveliest homes."

Helene tugged at Anne's sleeve. "The steamboat, the *Mary Powell*, will take us down. She is as grand as any hotel, with the finest salons. The people at St. Peter's make such a fuss over us. The women cook for days, coconut cakes and apple pies. Gallons of lemonade. And the music! Oh, wait till you hear the music! Jigs and reels to make your head swim. And we wear costumes. There'll be prizes for the one who is prettiest and the one who is funniest."

At first Anne demurred, but gave in to their persistence.

The following week, the excursionists clustered in St. Leo's churchyard as they waited for carriages that were hired to bring them to Newburg where the *Mary Powell* docked. Her father had shrugged when she mentioned the ham casserole he could warm for his dinner.

When Helene and Yvette first saw Anne, their eyes had widened. Anne knew they were impressed with her appearance, and she was relieved.

"You look perfectly beautiful," Helene cried. "Surely you will find a beau in Haverstraw."

It's my outfit that is beautiful, Anne told herself, as she recalled her father's harsh words from last Easter. "Your looks are finished...."

Still, only a year ago, Paul had told her she was lovely.

Anne had on a pale yellow taffeta, embroidered with lavender violets, her favorite silk gown. She hoped it would qualify as a costume. She was delighted to have an excuse to wear it, if only to a church dance, because it made Quebec come alive again. White kid gloves covered her arms past her elbows and hid her ragged nails and rough, reddened hands.

Yvette was dressed in black silk, her jacket decorated with jet beads. She had smudged coal dust beneath her eyes and from the corners of her nose to the corners of her lips. Wisps of floured hair escaped from a black bonnet to complete her transformation into an old woman.

Helene's dress was a garish orange, green, and red. A bright yellow turban hid her hair and ropes of colorful glass beads hung around her neck. Her cheeks were wildly rouged and her lips painted bright red. In her hand, she held a cup and saucer that contained dampened leaves of tea and she winked slyly when she offered to tell Anne her fortune. Anne was half-tempted to agree for she was anxious to learn what lay ahead.

Anne observed that neither woman had bothered to make herself look pretty. Was that because they were already married? Anne had put a lot of time into her appearance, with the thought that, as Helene had put it, she might find a beau in Haverstraw. She glanced across the churchyard to where her friends' husbands had joined the other men who all had a married look about them — bowler hats and dark brown or black suits, similar to what her father wore to church each Sunday. The men's posture, their turned backs, appeared to Anne an effort to avoid the wives who milled about the churchyard and greeted each other, often with explosions of laughter.

A solemn September sky threatened rain as Anne hurried up the gangplank of the *Mary Powell*. As she walked along the deck, adjusting her balance to the rocking of the boat, she noticed how much warmer the air was there at the river's edge. She was out of the dark clothing, and away from the farm.

The steamship had hardly left the dock at Newburg and begun to thread its way south through the narrow passage of the Hudson Highlands when rain began to pelt the partygoers. Everyone on deck scurried into the passenger lounges where they remained for the rest of the trip. Anne followed Helene and Yvette into a salon draped in burgundy velvet, reminiscent of her aunt's front parlor, and joined a group of older women. The younger women listened as the others discussed the merits of previous excursions. Nyack and Tarrytown were each delightful, but all agreed that Haverstraw was the best.

4

It was twilight by the time the *Mary Powell* docked at
Haverstraw. The rain had stopped and the air was moist and
fresh. The storm had blown eastward so that a shelf of clouds
clung to the top of the hills that lined the other side of the Hudson.
A welcoming party from the church had carriages waiting on
the Emeline Duck to bring their visitors to St. Peter's.

The carriages turned a corner and the tall steeple of St. Peter's
was silhouetted against the darkening sky. The men hollered and
the women clapped. When the carriages deposited them on the
sidewalk outside the huge brick church, the music from banjos
and fiddles called them inside. Anne's hesitation at being thrust
among strangers eased.

The church basement was festooned with garlands of apple-
green and pink crepe paper streamers. So many gas lamps lined
the walls that the room was lit as bright as day. Anne was seated
beside a table piled high with steaming casseroles, baskets and
platters filled with bread and meat. No one showed any interest
in the food.

Yvette and Helene had left to dance with their husbands and
Anne looked idly around the room. Directly across the dance
floor was an animated group of men, the tallest of whom had a
head covered with bright copper curls. The group cast furtive
glances her way as if they were discussing her. Anne looked away.

She wished she were able to flirt and entice a man's attention, but on the few occasions when she'd attempted to do this she felt so foolish that she soon gave it up. Instead, she turned her attention to the dancers and watched Helene and Yvette with their husbands appear and disappear in the throng.

Several of the Haverstraw men wore costumes. One was totally encased in a garment of looping brown yarn, his head covered by a hood from which two long, flapping ears dangled. From time to time, he barked and howled. Another man, short and slender, was dressed in a lacy white bridal gown and veil. His heavy work boots flashed as he twirled his partner around the floor.

The music reminded her of the French melodies she had grown up with in Biddeford. Lively, triple rhythms which teased taps from the toes of those who sat or stood along the walls.

Anne was unnerved and at the same time relieved when she noticed that the tall redhead had his eyes fixed on her as he wove his way across the dance floor. For a moment Anne thought he might be wearing a wig. Then she saw that his handlebar moustache and eyebrows were the same bright copper. His face, covered with freckles, wore a wide, open grin, so disarming that she smiled in response before either had said a word.

"I've taken a dare from my mates, so don't fail me," he pleaded. He bent forward in an outrageous bow, his right hand on his stomach, his left hand pressed against the middle of his back. A roar of laughter rose from the group across the floor.

He was a poor dancer who shuffled his feet with little attention to the music. As the evening wore on, she hardly noticed, for the fiddles and banjos quickened their pace, challenging the dancers, who yelled back at the music while they stamped and kicked and hurled themselves into a frenzied circle of legs and feet. Even those who only sat or stood, joined in the wildness with claps to the beat and pounding of their feet. He swept her around the floor so fast that she became dizzy and stumbled but his arm held her, even lifted her feet off the ground. Anne was caught up into the glorious turmoil and hooted foolishly along with the rest.

His name was Liam O'Connor, though his mates called him "Rusty," and he worked in the brickyards. His slight brogue reminded her of Biddeford.

"I'm with the group that came down from St. Leo's, up in Chestnut Grove," she told him.

"Say something more," he asked.

Confused at first, Anne realized he was fascinated by her accent. While she had studied English at the convent school in Biddeford, she had not used it in conversation until after she moved to Canada, and her accent was quite pronounced.

Liam stayed by her side for the rest of the evening, except briefly when, egged on by the crowd, he sang in a tenor voice both pleasant and strong, a plaintive ballad of a young musician heading off to war, while the unruly audience listened in silence. When people began to line up at the food table, he offered his arm.

"I'm too excited to eat, Liam. But you go ahead."

"And let some galoot come over here and steal my place?" he chortled, as he shook his head.

Liam told her he'd arrived in Haverstraw by chance. He was cutting ice down at Rockland Lake with some of the older boys from the Sparkill orphanage when, by luck, he found himself working alongside men from Curran's brickyard. Right away they knew he was from Connamara by his accent and when he told them he was looking for work they assured him he was as good as hired.

"Wait until the ice on the Hudson breaks up," they told him. "As soon as the barges can bring the bricks down river, the yards will be back in business." So he kept an eye on the river and, when he saw a fishing boat out in the channel, he snuck a pair of heavy boots and an extra mackinaw from the clothing room at the orphanage, and took off for Haverstraw. He was scattering sand and red ochre into brick molds by the next afternoon.

"Luck has followed me since the day I was born," he bragged.

It had been a long time since an attractive man had paid attention to her. Liam was not a likely beau. He was nowhere near as attractive as Paul. She suspected he might be much younger than she had first thought. She'd been misled by his height and the mustache. Anne did not ask his age for fear he might in turn inquire about hers.

"Why is it," she asked instead,"that so few men are in costume?"

"That's more for the women," he shrugged.

Back in Quebec City, where Anne had attended several masked balls, the men wore elaborate outfits, often outshining their wives, who mostly dressed in splendid gowns and hid behind feathered masks.

Her group from St. Leo's had begun to gather in order to catch the night boat back up river when, with a fanfare of ringing bells, a shrill woman's voice announced that the results were in from the judges and the awards ceremony was about to take place.

The man in the dog suit, amid roars of approval, received a ribbon for the funniest costume. Anne's cheeks flushed when she heard that hers had been chosen as the prettiest. Although the response from the crowd was more subdued than for the man, Anne could not help but notice when Liam's group of friends whistled, cheered, and stamped their feet in approval.

Word passed that they must hurry or they'd miss the night boat. Amid much bustle and shouting, their ever jovial hosts accompanied them to the waiting carriages, as women hugged each other with promises to keep in touch. Several men carried flaming pitch torches. They set out ahead of the carriages to light the way down to the Emeline Dock.

As Liam assisted Anne into one of the carriages, he asked,

"There's a dance here the Saturday before Advent. Should I look for you?"

Flattered, Anne asked, "Where is it you live?"

Startled, he paused before replying. "Curran's Boarding House on Allison Street."

"I'll write to you and let you know." she called out, as the carriage pulled away.

In the flickering light of the torches, as the darkness closed in around him, the grin on Liam's face was drawn into a puzzled frown.

Later, in the less elaborate salon of the night boat the older women nodded knowingly, while Helene teased Anne.

"You'll soon be rocking a little one with lovely copper curls."

"And," Yvette added, "when he's old enough to understand, we'll tell him all about it. Of the night his mother was voted the prettiest woman at the dance and a tall redheaded stranger, once he set eyes on her, didn't leave her side for the rest of the evening."

5

Ned Walsh had drifted along behind a crowd of fellow Irishmen when they climbed aboard a schooner on its return trip to Haverstraw, in search of jobs in the brickyards. But when Tim Maloney, the chief foreman at the Curran yard, happened to be climbing the clay bank and watched Ned collapse into a half-filled cart, he shook his head. "He'll never make it here," he told himself. A man needed a strong, muscular back to work in a brickyard. To dig out the heavy clay, shovel it into the horse-drawn carts, lift moulds packed with the wet clay and empty them onto the smoothed bed of the yard where they could dry in the sun, then toss the green bricks up to other men who formed them into huge arched kilns to be burned, and finally loaded the fired bricks onto barges and schooners. A man had to be strong.

As Tim Maloney walked over to Ned to fire him, he remembered what Liz Farrelly had confided to him a few days earlier: "Unless I can find another pair of hands, I'll have to cut back on my meals to the yards." Liz was an excellent cook, and regularly supplied hot breakfasts and dinners to the workers.

So he gave Ned his walking papers and Liz Farrelly's address.

Liz Farrelly ran a saloon over on Broad Street, a favorite haven for Curran men. On a Sunday morning some years back, while the rest of his family dressed for church, her husband led their carriage around to the front of the house and, somehow, as he held the bridle and waited for them, the horse kicked him in the chest. By the time he was lifted onto a wagon and rushed down to Nyack Hospital, he was dead.

Liz sold their large home up on Hudson Avenue, and the two schooners that her husband had recently purchased, and invested the proceeds in a smaller house closer to the river, on Broad Street. She kept the upstairs rooms for her three children and herself, and converted the first floor into a grocery and the basement into a saloon. When the workers discovered how well she filled a meal pail, she was overwhelmed with orders.

Before the day was over, Ned had packed his few belongings and departed the over-crowded boarding house, and had taken up residence in a small room off Liz Farrelly's kitchen. His bedroom was spotless, a refreshing contrast to the foul-smelling boarding house, and restored in him a sense of privacy he had not experienced since leaving his tiny room in the seminary. That night, Liz set a place for him at the supper table, and told her three children to call him Uncle Ned. Unused to the company of children, and initially leery, he was pleased to discover that her five-year-old son, Robert, as well as Kate, six, and Theresa, eight, although lively, were well-mannered. The kitchen was remarkably clean and orderly despite the volume of food that passed through it. Pots of red geraniums on the sills of two crisply curtained windows put him in mind of his mother's home.

At Farrelly's, the nightly debate had begun to rock the saloon. Ned Walsh, behind the bar, only half-listened as he wiped away cigar ashes and mopped up slopped ale. Without fail, the men dug about until a topic was found on which they could disagree. Often, the debate started in a small group clustered around the billiard table or perhaps between two men, a pint of beer clutched in one hand, while the other, at the end of a stiffened arm, was propped against the stone wall of the cellar. As tonight, when a sufficiently controversial topic surfaced, the whole saloon was engaged and sides formed quickly. In no time at all, the dispute reached a pitch sufficiently fevered to burn from their minds the tedious, backbreaking day they had just completed in the clay pits. They were a raucous, rough bunch, but they abided by Liz Farrelly's rule against brawling and kept their fists to themselves. Inside her saloon, they did. Tonight, Ned thought, might be the exception. For the topic was clay.

Ned removed empty pints from the bar, avoiding any that held even a drop of beer, and carefully buried them in the tub of sudsy water at his feet. Tonight there could be trouble, for it was not an even match. Sides were predictably drawn, according to where you worked. A few, like Barney Cox, were employed at the stone quarry. The rest of them in brickyards.

Men who worked in Curran's, a major brickyard on the river, often found themselves on the defensive when the subject under discussion was clay, because Curran was notorious for his encroachment on property lines which undermined a neighbor's claybank. The heavy blue clay inevitably tumbled away from the neighbor and onto Curran's land and was immediately scooped up into horse-drawn carts and hauled over to the mixing machine, before any warrant could be prepared, much less delivered to Michael Curran.

"Ah, sure everyone knows how Curran plays the game. Always digs so close to the line that our clay falls into his yard."

"If it's on our land, it's our clay," insisted broad-shouldered Tim Maloney. His tone declared the argument finished.

As if a particle of that land is his, Ned thought. The loyalty the workers felt for their yard was remarkable. They stuck together like they were family, and would leave one yard for another only after they'd been fired, usually for missing work after a very wet weekend.

"Gravity is an act of God," Maloney declared.

It amused Ned how frequently God was brought up to settle a discussion. Ned doubted that any of these hard-playing men rose early enough on a Sunday morning to attend church. Still, God had the final word.

As for the clay—clay was Haverstraw Gold. Fine blue clay, sandwiched between layers of even finer sand left behind after the glaciers ground their way through the Hudson Valley hills and then receded. When it was cooked into bricks and shipped down the river to New York, Haverstraw's clay brought a pretty penny. Not to the yard workers, of course, who were lucky if they earned $1.25 a day for their backbreaking efforts.

Ned pulled another pint for Tim Maloney, but avoided his eye, for he wanted no part of this argument.

Haverstraw was the capital of the brick-making world, its residents claimed. Every year, more than a million bricks were stacked on schooners or sloops, but mostly on barges. Floated down the river, then off-loaded onto city docks and into hods, which other brawny shoulders hauled up rickety ladders that swayed and groaned beneath the weight.

New York had a voracious appetite. There was no end in sight for its demand for bricks. It had already rebuilt the skyline a fire had consumed half a century ago. And relentlessly inched northward. Orchards and pastures, brooks and streams were replaced by block after block of buildings. Brick buildings that would never burn down. Small wonder clay was gold.

"Schoolmaster Walsh, you can settle it." Often, when an argument lagged, they turned to Ned.

Most of the men had nicknames. Ned's was Schoolmaster. After Ned had started to work at Farrelly's, now and then they overheard him mention a piece of history, like the Battle of the Boyne, or mention one of the myths or kings dear to their hearts, like Cuchilaine and Maeve. That sort of thing. Somehow they figured out he wasn't showing off, not even aware how impressed they were until they teased him. He'd shrug it off if someone said he'd been seen leaving the village library. Soon they decided he was like a teacher back in Ireland and they trusted what he said.

They accepted him and he became the Schoolmaster. They

knew he was from Belfast and that was enough.

Ned was not ready to speak about his six years at Sacred Heart Seminary. On nights when he could not sleep, his mind picked over those six years and searched for an answer to why he'd been denied ordination.

"Do you think you could help me out, Mr. Walsh?" A young redhead Ned had seen often in Farrelly's spoke in a low voice and gestured for Ned to accompany him to a quiet corner of the room.

"Just a moment," Ned told him, and turned back to the crowd, which waited for his decision.

"What about the courts? What do the courts say?" Ned asked.

A volley of oaths and similar petitions for divine intercession followed.

"The courts?" Jimmy Kelleher's scornful voice carried above the others. "When Curran's brother owns the largest bank in town, and their cousin has been state senator for fifteen years…." The curses grew more intense.

"No, no, listen to him. Hear the man out," Will Nolan shouted. The voices subsided.

Ned continued, carefully, quietly. "Didn't the courts settle the matter? The owner of a yard is entitled to whatever clay may fall from another yard."

"It's stealing, that's what it is. Outright stealing!"

"And what about people like me?" demanded John Joe McGrath. "My home is about to fall into the pit. They dig closer and closer each day. My wife swears she can feel it shaking." John Joe had been waging a private battle with Curran for years with no success.

Will Nolan was ready. "Curran will buy your house tomorrow, and you know it. We all know it."

Cheers and boos rocked the room.

Ned grimaced, spreading his palms in a futile gesture. Nothing would be settled here tonight. He pulled a pint for a new customer, then left the fray to join the young man who waited for him in a dimly lit area where the bar joined the back wall.

With a sheepish grin, the redhead introduced himself, "I'm Liam O'Connor, Mr. Walsh, though everybody calls me Rusty. And— I'm not a great one for reading."

Who in this crowd is? Ned thought to himself. One or two maybe. Now and then he had heard the boy silence the saloon with his clear tenor voice, as he sang familiar ballads from the other side. Probably, the lad wanted something read to him. Ned expected some sort of legal document or perhaps a letter from Ireland, and was surprised when the boy handed him a pale blue envelope, addressed in a delicate script.

Liam was still grinning. "It's from a girl. She lives on a farm up the river in Chestnut Grove. You may remember, the night the mates were giving me such a hard time?"

Ned vaguely remembered an evening when the saloon had buzzed for awhile with crude but good-natured kidding about Rusty and a girl at a dance. He pictured a giggling, fresh-faced young woman.

Her name was Anne Beauvois and her note said the dance had been lovely. She regretted that she could not attend the pre-Advent dance.

"Do you think I could send her an answer? I mean, would you write one for me, Mr. Walsh?"

A few weeks later, the boy came back to Ned with the same sheepish grin and another pale blue envelope. Again, Ned read the letter and helped Liam invent a reply. Liam started to call him Ned, instead of Mr. Walsh, but never Schoolmaster and Ned never called Liam Rusty. It was while the two of them were working on the third reply that Ned wondered if what he was doing was honest. He said so to Liam and suggested they explain that his penmanship was not the best, and that a friend had been helping him out.

But Liam was adamant. "Later, when she knows me better. And where's the harm in it, after all?"

Over the past year, at least six or seven of the men had come to Ned for help, as Liam had, although this was the only time a girl was involved. Back in his seminary days, where the core of studies was philosophy and theology, Ned had frequently been assigned to tutor the slower boys, and he did this gladly. He had considered it part of his preparation to become a missionary.

Ned never had a conversation with a girl, much less written a letter to one before he entered the seminary. His sister, Kathleen, did not count. He had missed his mother dreadfully at first, and would whisper a silent goodnight to her before he dropped off to sleep. He confided this to his spiritual director, who counseled him that the Rule did not allow such thoughts. The Rule promised freedom from all earthly attachments and would enable him to totally serve God. After much prayer and struggle, that night did come; he was able to turn his face toward the wall next to his bed, his mind empty of any thought of his mother.

6

Anne was not certain why she'd asked Liam for his address. She suspected it might have been a reluctance to allow the magic of the evening to fade. Liam O'Connor was amusing but would not make a suitable husband. He was coarse, too brash, and worked in a brickyard. And he was Irish.

Nonetheless, as soon as she slid the paring knife under the flap of his letter, for a brief instant she could hear the fiddles and was back whirling about.

Liam's neat, firm hand, his faultless spelling and grammar, impressed Anne. There evidently was more to him than than she had observed. His signature was an amusing caricature of his name; she could imagine him grinning as he drew it.

While Anne went about tending the chickens, collecting eggs, sweeping the slate floor of the cabin, her determination to leave her father grew. Her chances of finding a husband would be better if she concealed everything about Quebec and presented herself as the daughter of a farmer who had recently moved to Chestnut Grove from a mill town in Maine. She would practice her deception on this laborer from Haverstraw, and, by the time a more suitable candidate turned up, she would be less likely to make a slip.

Anne quickly dismissed any misgivings she had about dishonesty. She would carefully avoid any outright lies.

The following day, after Anne had served her father his dinner of boiled cabbage and ham, she took her writing tablet and bottle of ink outside into the sunshine. She made herself comfortable on the plank bench, raised her face to the warmth, and breathed in the crisp November air, grateful it was not raining.

In her next letter, Anne tried to recapture the sense of happy expectation over the approach of Christmas that she and her brothers and her friends had shared back in Biddeford. Last year, she and her father did not celebrate Christmas; their despair over the absence of her mother had stripped life down to its bare essentials.

Anne wrote of trips into the woods to gather red berries and pine boughs to place around the cabin. And hours spent mincing the ingredients for the *tourtières*, the traditional pork and spice pies that her father liked. Although she did not have a knack for pie crusts and hers were a dreadful patchwork, several raisin and sugar pies had already been baked and wrapped, and were stored in the unheated shed, in the hope that Christmas visitors might drop by. Anne did not mention that her father scowled when she asked him to buy extra sugar and spices. Instead, she told of her father cutting down a spruce tree, which she dressed with brightly colored ribbons and strings of popcorn and berries. Beneath it lay her mother's treasured *crêche*.

As Anne wrote, pleasant images filled her mind of Christmas Eve pageants at St. Andre's Church in Biddeford, where every child was either a shepherd or an angel unless, if they were tall, Mary and Joseph. The fear-tinged excitement when, on the dot of midnight, the church was plunged into darkness. Year after year, the same delight after the candles were relit, and they saw the manger was no longer empty. Then, back home again, her mother smiling when Anne and her brothers discovered oranges and candy hidden behind the *crêche*, during the *reveillon*.

Or the chill quiet of a Quebec night. Setting out into the darkness for Midnight Mass, tucked warmly in a sleigh between her aunt and uncle, the horses' hooves muffled as they flew over the packed snow; the black velvet night embroidered with lights of candles in windows, guiding the Christ Child. Aunt Josie's house, filled with the scent of balsam, with holly and evergreen boughs, pine cones, and the glow of candles that gleamed and flickered on shining mahogany.

7

The Christmas goose, a gift from Mr. Lessard, stuffed, trussed, and covered with a piece of cloth soaked with melted butter, and slowly roasting in the brick oven, filled the cabin with a mouth-watering aroma. Although it was only her father and herself, Anne had decided to make the best of things and create a special meal.

She stepped outside the stuffy cabin to escape the heat of the oven. During the night, a new fall of snow had covered over the ugliness of the farmyard, except for the steaming dung heap. The morning sky, deep blue and cloudless, was fringed by tips of hemlock and spruce for as far as she could see. From behind the barn where they kept the chickens, she heard a rooster announce himself and, for no reason, this made Anne smile.

If her father had not insisted that he would spend Christmas at his own table, they could both be over at Helene's house, and he might have been temporarily roused from his bad temper by the companionship of her friend's older husband. Helene's mother and aunt, who arrived yesterday for the holiday, would help with the preparations for the dinner. Anne had discovered that when women worked together it became an enjoyable time of story-telling and laughter. Even scouring pots in someone else's kitchen could become a pleasant experience.

Anne had just seated herself on the narrow outside bench

when she noticed movement down near the main road where their lane began, and saw the figure of a man headed toward their cabin. A tramp seeking a bit of food. She said a quick prayer that her father, in the spirit of Christmas, would not roar for him to get off the property but instead invite him to share their meal. While these thoughts passed through Anne's head, the man drew closer. When she saw the lock of copper hair that escaped from the hood of his jacket, she realized it was Liam O'Connor. His cheeks were red from the cold.

"Where in the world…?" Anne's astonishment froze her for a moment. Then she ran to him and drew him inside the cabin. Her father, seated next to the fireplace with a tangled bundle of wire to be untwisted, looked up. His eyes narrowed when he saw Anne was not alone.

She pulled a chair close to the fire for the shivering young man, and turned to her father. "*Ici, Liam, mon père.*"

In answer to the question in Liam's eyes, Anne apologized. "We speak French to each other. My father understands some English but he prefers French."

"Isn't it grand in here," Liam sniffed as he pulled off his jacket. "Is that your famous meat pie I'm smelling?"

"The *tourtière*?" She smiled for she remembered describing it in her last letter. "No, that's the goose. Dinner will be ready in an hour or so."

This was such an unexpected turn of events. Anne was delighted to see him, to have a visitor in their home on Christmas.

"Tell me how you found us? How far did you walk in this cold?"

"At the Chestnut Grove Station, I asked for the Beauvois farm. It was only a skip and a jump from there. Scarcely worth the price of a horse." A trace of bravado in his manner made him sound like a young boy.

"Six miles, at least," Anne scolded, "in such weather."

"Home in Ireland," he shrugged, "we'd walk twice that and

not give it a thought.

"When you wrote about all the food you were making, in case friends dropped by, I couldn't resist. I had to have a taste of that meat pie."

"My *tourtière*," Anne laughed, nodding to her father, trying to include him in the conversation. She knew he was listening, taking everything in.

Her father raised an eyebrow and asked with a mocking note in his voice. "*Maudit Irlandais?*" The name the Biddeford French had for their Irish neighbors: goddam Irish.

Anne abbreviated the translation for Liam's benefit.

"Irish," she nodded

Back in Biddeford, the French and Irish worked side by side, shopped in each other's stores and generally got along. However, a French girl had better not be caught spending time with an Irish boy. Not only would her family object; she would be shunned by her entire neighborhood. Today, it did not matter to Anne whether her father approved of Liam or not. Ever since Easter, when she found the nerve to tell him that she was returning to Quebec, a sort of truce had set in. Then, after Aunt Josie died, Anne discovered she no longer wanted anyone else's approval. She was on her own now.

"Oh, yes—I'm from the Emerald Isle," Liam chortled.

An uncomfortable pause followed, neither man said anything. Anne suspected her father was confused by Liam's cheerfulness.

"Papa," she suggested, "why don't you take Liam out to the barn, while I finish dinner?"

It was more than an hour before the two men returned.

"Did you walk every foot of the farm?" Anne asked them playfully. Liam must have displayed considerable interest in everything her father showed him, because the older man's manner was noticeably warmer. He took Liam's jacket and gave him a slap on the shoulder.

Liam's presence at the Christmas meal dispelled her father's customary black mood.

Holding his knife and fork in mid-air, her father raised his chin, gesturing toward Liam.

"A hard worker."

He pointed his knife toward Liam's plate.

"His hands." He nodded approvingly. Her father's ultimate measure of a man, a willingness to work hard.

Liam caught on despite the language difference and raised his hands proudly. They were callused and scarred, the knuckles crusted with scabs. Red dust outlined his fingernails. Anne had not noticed Liam's hands before this. At the dance, she'd worn her gloves to conceal her split and torn nails but had given no thought to his.

When Liam asked for a third helping of goose, Anne felt rewarded for all her efforts. She was grateful when he declined another serving of the *tourtière*. Her father, apparently relived that the pie would remain only half eaten, and it would be his dinner the following day, in rare good humor urged Liam on with "*Bourre-toi...bourre-toi.*" To stuff himself. Liam had won her father's approval.

8

The bottles of whiskey and rum that stood behind the bar in Farrelly's needed dusting. As did everything else that stayed still for a moment in Haverstraw, Ned thought. The mildest wind lifted any particles of clay or red ochre that were carried out of the brickyards on jackets and boots, eyebrows and beards, and scattered them throughout the village. Entering the slightest crack between window sash and frame, invading every house, every building in Haverstraw, even, he had heard, carpeting the verandas of the fine homes up the hill on Hudson Avenue. Farrelly's had more than its share of grime, down here in the cellar, with its particular clientele. Liz somehow kept the dust out of her kitchen despite the grocery's parade of boots.

Ned kept a vigilant eye on the mirror behind the bottles, as he wiped away the dust with a damp rag. The nightly swirl of oaths and shouted outrage easily ignited fists.

Tonight the uproar was over a story Tim Maloney read to them from the local paper. Two women had been arrested up in Goshen, some twenty miles northwest of Haverstraw. The women had invaded a saloon and refused to leave and, instead, knelt in the sawdust singing verses from "Father, Dear Father, Come Home To Us Now," a sentimental temperance ballad, until the police arrived. Tim Maloney waved the newspaper aloft as he recounted the facts.

Man's God-given right to a pint was under attack. For once, no sides were taken. The argument boiled around how to respond. Some men were prepared to hire horses and take off for Goshen. Find the jail where the women were being held. What would follow was not clear or not expressed. Others focused on schemes to prevent such women from entering Haverstraw.

"Hang them," cried a young man in a derby hat, as he looked about for allies. He was either unheard or ignored. The attention of the preoccupied throng bounced and scattered.

Ned had often led drunken men home to furious, despairing wives and he shared a degree of sympathy with the crusaders. He was uncertain how to respond should he be drawn into the ruckus. However, his opinion was not solicited. Tim Maloney rallied thunderous approval when he bellowed over the din, "Women have no place talking about, much less deciding, if, when, or where, a man can take a drink. We will not allow this." The room exploded with roars of agreement and the thunder of feet .

Liz Farrelly, her hair in curling rags, poked her head down from the top of the cellar stairs, alarm on her face.

"Is it a hanging they're after?" she shouted to Ned through the racket.

"Go on to bed, " he reassured her. " It's just the boyos having their rare bit of fun."

Liz shrugged, nodded, and disappeared.

Ned sighed as he began to tidy up. It was time to close the bar, and extra effort on his part would be required to quiet this crowd down and get them out and up into the backyard.

As Ned reached up to close the slanted cellar door, he realized Liam stood waiting at the bar. Wearily, Ned went over to him.

"Not tonight. Tomorrow. Come early."

"I've got grand news." His eyes danced, his lips pressed tight.

Ned's mother would say Liam looked like the cat that ate the canary.

"Tomorrow," Ned repeated.

When Liam stopped by Farrelly's after work the next day, he found Ned upstairs in the grocery busily measuring pound sacks of sugar from a large white bag propped against a barrel of apples.

"Mr. Curran has offered me a loan. He says McCauley's widow has to sell shares in her husband's schooner. Mike McNabb and me, we're going to buy in.

"I'm on my way. This is the first step. Come in with us, Ned. We'll be partners."

Liam had grand plans for himself and was forever telling anyone who'd listen, how he'd soon have his own brickyard, his own boats. "I'll be down in New York City with the best of them. Calling the shots, making the deals, and the money spilling out of my pockets."

Ned banked most of his wages each week, as he had little need for money. But he had no desire to invest his small savings in a brick schooner. After visiting Dublin, Liverpool, and London, he agreed with Liam that New York, filled with a glut of activity and raw energy, held a special and contagious excitement. But for Ned, there was nothing about any city that could match the sight of a blazing sun as it slowly climbed above the rounded hills beyond Haverstraw Bay.

"Mr. Curran has had his eye on me. Could you believe that? Mr. Curran. Knows I never miss a payday at the bank. Even knows how much is in my account. Mr. Curran says I have vision. I'm the kind of man he likes to help."

The Currans had the power in Haverstraw. One was president of Rockland Savings Bank, his brother was owner of the brickyard where Liam worked, and the Chief of Police was brother to them both. Ned suspected that whatever was being offered to Liam would benefit Mr. Curran more than it would his friend.

Liam drew out from inside his shirt a small leather pouch which hung from his neck on a slender, braided cord. "It's my veil. It marked me as special the day I was born."

Ned was a small boy when he first heard talk about a caul, a veil. The membrane that sometimes covered the face of a new-born child. He once heard of a fisherman who carried a corner of his son's caul as protection from drowning.

He jiggled the pouch at Ned, then tucked it back inside his shirt. "My friend, before you stands a man with a future."

9

It was early in the night, the saloon was quiet. Over in the corner, three customers huddled around a game of poker, their voices low, oblivious to the two men at the bar.

As Ned read the girl's letter to Liam, he felt certain that the limits of decency had been exceeded in the previous letter. Liam bragged that he'd been promoted to foreman. Untrue and also unlikely, for the position of foreman went to older, more seasoned workers. Liam had overcome Ned's objections with cajolery, "Isn't it all just fun. Where's the harm of it, after all?"

Despite himself, Ned could not help wondering about the girl. A bit of a ninny, overturning pails of milk. The neatness of her penmanship puzzled him. The perfect strokes and swirls. Her clever description of an owl's cry surpassed what he expected from a farm girl. When Ned compared her to the young seminarians he had tutored, their hands still callused from the plow, struggling and stumbling over the simplest words, he was perplexed. Intrigued, if he was honest about it.

Ned rested his left elbow on the bar, his chin propped on his fist, ink and paper in front of him, the pen poised in his other hand. He waited as Liam scoured his thoughts for a reply. While Ned waited for the young man to speak, a simple solution came to him, one that could solve his dilemma. He would teach Liam to write. Write his own letters.

Ned placed the pen on the bar and, with quiet firmness, addressed the young man. "Listen to me."

The note of authority in Ned's voice interrupted Liam's intense concentration.

Ned said, "This is the last letter I'll do for you, unless you agree to let me teach you how to write."

A wave of panic flashed across Liam's face. "But that's it. I have no mind for it. I'm thick. Back at the orphanage, when they found out I didn't read, I was put with the young ones. The older boys would hold their noses and crow that I still wet my britches. I was in a fight every day over it. It didn't matter how often the teacher rapped me with the ruler, I just couldn't learn. I can do my sums and write my name, and that's all."

Liam tried to smile, to erase the memory, and finally, the familiar grin broke through. "That's it," he bragged. "I'm just thick."

Ned waited, his chin once more on his upraised fist. Liam's lips pursed as he collected his next thought. His eyes began to dance.

"Tell her...." He stammered, hesitated, then blurted it out. "Tell her, I want to marry her."

Stunned, Ned's fist fell away from his chin. He raised his head, his mouth open in amazement. It was one thing for Liam to pretend he was a foreman. But this, this was too much.

"You don't mean it. You want to marry her?" Ned was incredulous.

The three men in the corner tilted their faces toward the bar, listening, their interest piqued. A glare from Ned sent them back to their card game.

These letters were a game. They were nonsense. Liam wove his daydreams, and Ned scribbled them down. Ned understood why the men needed their games, needed some relief from the tedium of the clay, the mindless hours of digging, dumping, then hauling, day after day, with never a diversion.

Small wonder they needed their games.

Liam leaned closer to Ned. "Mr. Curran says a man with a

wife is the best worker. He's dependable. He can be counted on." He added, a boyish pride in his voice, "Didn't I tell you—he's got his eye on me?"

Liam had decided to marry Anne in order to impress Mr. Curran.

Ned fought a moment of panic, a desperate wish to retrieve the letters. To somehow unravel the correspondence, as he had so often watched his mother pull apart a knitted garment and gather the yarn back into a ball.

"That settles it. I'm finished with this. Find someone else to write your letters."

Crestfallen, Liam's cocky manner evaporated.

"No, no. I could never do that. Never. I couldn't let on to anyone else."

A tense silence hung between them. The men in the corner stared over their cards as Liam's confidence began to return. "And what's wrong with my marrying her? I'd make a fine husband. I work hard, save my money. And I don't mess around with women. What else do I need...?" His voice trailed away, a look of bewilderment in his eyes.

Ned had long ago put away thoughts of marriage, after it was settled that he would join the Order. At fifteen, once the decision had been made, and it had not seemed an enormous decision at the time, he eagerly accepted the rules and practices that would lead him to the priesthood. More difficult by far was later on, after he returned to the world, the world of women. Six years apart from women had left him unprepared. The problem now was not with the older ones, like Liz Farrelly. It was the younger ones who came into the store, whose glances questioned him in ways that made his cheeks burn. The fact was, they frightened him. That was the truth of it. He could not return their smiles; his face would stiffen, and he would respond brusquely, if at all, miserable and shamed by his rudeness.

As he listened to the young man's list of qualifications, Ned had to admit that Liam might have the makings of a husband. Nursing the one pint every evening, wouldn't spend the money on a second. No sign of rowdiness. But Liam was only a boy, not even twenty. Still, as Ned reflected further, he'd known of men choosing wives as casually as if they were buying a horse or a pair of new boots. But Ned had played no part in those situations. Was not involved in any way, was not responsible. This was different.

"All right," he conceded. "But we must tell her a friend has been helping with the letters."

"Not yet. Not yet. There's time for that later," Liam pleaded. "Let's see if she'll have me, first."

Ned's shoulders sagged as he slowly shook his head from side to side in a hopeless protest.

"You're a grand fellow, just grand," Liam crowed.

Ned sent Liam on his way with a promise that the letter would be ready the following afternoon.

Ned sat at the kitchen table, worrying a thread in his cuff. The house was quiet, Liz and the children long in their beds. He was tired and his back ached from having lifted crates of potatoes and onions earlier in the day. He knew better than to put off the letter. Get it done and off his mind, or else it would nag at him and keep him from sleep.

Why had he let things go this far? It had been a lark, at first. An amusement. Perhaps he was foolish to worry. Why would the girl agree to so important a step on the basis of the few letters they had exchanged? He absentmindedly scribbled some letters at the top of the page, noticed what he had done and winced. "A.M.D.G." Where did that come from, after all these years? He turned to find a clean piece of paper and decided against it. The inscription would hold no meaning for the girl. A devotional practice taught in the seminary, to inscribe A.M.D.G. at the top of each page of work. *Ad Majorem Dei Gloriam*. A reminder that all of one's work was consecrated to God.

And suddenly he remembered the day he found himself out on a cobblestone pavement, a five-pound note in the inside pocket of his ill-fitting black suit, a set of clean underwear and a pair of socks in the cardboard suitcase that dangled from his left hand. Bewildered, not yet furious. Unable to comprehend how his future, even his past, had been erased. A week before the ceremony, summoned and told he would not be ordained. Denied an explanation. It had been decided and was not to be questioned.

Certain, until he heard the huge iron gate lock behind him, that it would all be cleared up. Assured by his spiritual advisor that a mistake had been made, letters were sent to the head of the Order, even to Rome, requesting consideration, the opportunity to defend himself from unspoken charges, unknown accusations. No replies, no clarification, only word passed along through classmates that he was making a nuisance of himself. And drumming through his thoughts, the specter of a failed vocation. Unspeakable, unforgivable. A cause for damnation. The loss of his soul.

Ned chided himself for again dwelling on what he had learned to dismiss. He shook his head and returned to the letter.

Ned rubbed his hands up his cheeks and across his eyebrows to chase the weariness, and reread what he had written. The proposal was as straightforward and blunt as he could craft it. "I am asking you to marry me and look forward to your acceptance." Since Liam had explained his purpose, Ned avoided any hint of sentiment. Angry at himself as much as Liam, Ned folded the missive and tucked it unsigned in his pocket, ready for Liam's signature. From the very first, he had insisted Liam scratch his name at the bottom of every letter.

10

It had been a miserable week for Anne. Hurrying with a basket of wet wash to make the most of the midday sun, she had tripped over the handle of a hoe and had fallen, the palm of her right hand braced before her to protect the clean clothes from the muddy ground. That was five days ago, but her wrist still hurt, so that she had to hold it close to her waist while she worked. It took forever to crank the butter churn with her left hand, to peel and chop onions and carrots for dinner. The warm June days caused her hair to cling to her neck and, with only one hand available, the pins she used to fasten it into a bun repeatedly fell out.

The discomfort from her wrist aggravated her already miserable state of mind, the result of a recent letter from Louise. Anne had recognized her friend's childish script and quickly tore open the envelope. She had hurried out of the cabin to sit on the outside bench where she could read in the full light of the afternoon.

It was a horrid letter.

Louise wrote that Anne would not be teaching in any school that the nuns supervised. The curé in Quebec City had somehow learned the identity of Anne's companion that Sunday afternoon, when she and Paul had passed him on the *terrasse Dufferin*, and he wasted no time notifying the Mother General that one of her teachers was seen in the company of a married man. Having received this scandalous news, she quickly assured the curé that such a woman would never put a foot in one of her classrooms. The news had traveled south with the nuns who made regular train trips to Biddeford. Parishioners, gathered on the front steps of St. Andre's after Mass, shook their heads and exchanged sighs of relief that Anne's mother had died before witnessing her daughter's fall from grace. Louise's father forbade any further contact her so this would have to be her last letter.

Anne ran back inside the cabin and up to her cot on the loft and lay there in the shadows, curled in a ball, arms around her knees, her eyes closed. *He's not a married man. He's divorced.*

They had met in a bookstore in Quebec City, in the Lower Town beneath the Terrace. Anne, seeking a Jane Austin novel, had sought help from a clerk who quickly located several among the English collection. Her uncle's library was lined with more volumes than she could ever read but she had not found any by this favorite author.

After selecting *Pride and Prejudice,* she inquired about the price, mimicking Uncle Henri's manner when addressing servants. This would be the first book she'd ever bought, and she wished to conceal that fact..

"It is in English," the clerk had cautioned her.

"Of course," she replied brusquely.

"Forgive me,' the clerk said gently, "but it is unusual for a young woman to purchase a book written in English."

Anne, disarmed by his apology and ashamed at her pompous manner, looked directly at the clerk for the first time. He was older than she, perhaps twenty-five or maybe thirty. His sad, gray eyes, and the hesitant slant of his head, seemed to anticipate further reprimand from Anne. She wanted to make amends.

"When we studied Miss Austin in school, her stories were poked at and pulled apart and made into lessons. I've longed to read her quietly, not worrying about why or how things were written."

He laughed pleasantly. "You are no longer a student?"

"I am a teacher." She suddenly wanted to impress this handsome young man. "At a school in the parish of Beaupré." She did not add that the school was a single room in a tiny building, that that the pay was minimal and she boarded with farm families.

"And do you visit the Shrine there?"

"Every July 26th, on St. Anne's feast day. A promise I made to my mother."

"Someday, I hope to see it," he said.

It was a month later, after she had left the train at Beaupré and joined the throng of pilgrims, many on crutches or in wheel chairs, streaming toward the Basilica, when she recognized Paul standing in front of the enormous structure. Although she was delightedly surprised, she restrained the smile that sprang to her lips, striving for decorum and sophistication. Paul tipped his hat and nodded at her. His sad eyes were grave.

"Thank heavens. In this immense crowd, I despaired of ever finding you. I had no idea there would be so many people."

His remark satisfied her hope that this was not an accidental encounter.

Together, they entered the Basilica and found space in one of the rear pews. Anne's thoughts were filled with questions and wonder. How did this come about, with no effort on her part? No devious plotting or scheming. This handsome and intelligent man at her elbow. If only the girls from school could see her. And, how fortunate that she was wearing her new gown, the one with lace and pink roses.

Later Anne realized, after Mass was over and they had left the church, distracted by Paul's presence, she had not properly thanked St. Anne for her help and protection during the past year. Nor sought it for the next. Anne told Paul she had forgotten something, and would be right back. She hurried inside to the statue of St. Anne holding her daughter, Mary, knelt before it, silently offered her prayers of thanksgiving and petition, and then returned to Paul.

Uncertain whether or not he planned to immediately leave Beaupré, she suggested they might visit the Scala Santa on the hill behind the Basilica, on the Avenue Royale.

"Of course. Of course. I want to see everything."

As they approached the white clapboard building, Anne explained that the Scala was a devotion which represented the twenty-eight steps which Jesus, during his Passion, had mounted on his way to Pontius Pilate. Paul gestured toward the men and women who were ascending the steep flight of stairs on their knees.

"Have you climbed these steps on your knees?"

"Once with my mother, when I was young. You recite a special prayer on each step."

After a few moments, she turned away and exclaimed, "I am famished. I've had no breakfast." Anne had fasted since the previous evening in order to receive Communion.

At a nearby inn, a boisterous group of pilgrims invited Paul and Anne to join their table. Anne found she was able to speak with them and Paul in an easy and familiar manner, as she might have spoken with Louise or Aunt Josie, and was secretly amazed, for she had never before sat alone like this with strangers, especially with a handsome young man who had taken a train to find her. Lively and contagious laughter flowed easily among them. It was the most exciting day of Anne's life. Her previous pilgrimages to the Shrine had always been solemn and prayerful occasions, while today's had turned into a joyous celebration, a holiday.

Paul hired a *calèche* to bring them back to Quebec City. He wanted to hear all about her childhood in Biddeford and what her plans were for the rest of the summer. He seemed interested in everything about her. Hours seemed like minutes and then they were in front of Aunt Josie's, the driver waiting while Paul assisted her from the two-wheeled carriage.

"Have you seen *la Chute-Montmorency?*"

Anne said she had only glimpsed the falls at Montmorency from the train on her weekly trips to and from Beaupré.

"Would you like to visit them next Sunday?" he asked.

During the following week, whether she was sharing meals with her aunt and uncle, or visiting with school friends, or selecting skirts and shirtwaists for the fall, her thoughts returned to Paul. Paul — a perfect name for a man. As she repeated it over and over again to herself, his solemn gray eyes flashed before her. I'm no longer a girl, she thought. I have begun my new life as a woman.

As she related to Aunt Josie how Paul had shown up at the basilica, and how attractive and well mannered he was, she became aware of excitement rising in her voice and suspected her aunt might be restraining an indulgent smile. Embarrassed and determined to say no more for the moment, she excused herself and hurried to her room. But she longed to tell somebody about this handsome young man.

Sunday, after she had introduced Paul to her aunt and uncle, he sat with them in the parlor and exchanged impressions of the Montmorency Falls, comparing them favorably with Niagara's. Aunt Josie invited Paul to join them for dinner the following Saturday. Anne sent her a quick, grateful glance.

The sky above the St. Lawrence was leaden and the air warm. It might rain, Anne thought, and, if it did, the open carriage Paul had hired would offer no shelter. But she would not let rain or anything else to spoil this perfect day.

They left the horse and carriage and proceeded toward the funicular railway which would carry them up the side of the steep cliff. Anne suppressed her terror as the elevator ground its noisy, lurching way up the slope. When the small wooden car finally reached the top, and Paul was assisting her out onto the platform, she sighed with relief.

They continued the rest of the climb on foot, following a narrow path along the west side of the cliff until they reached a suspension bridge stretching above the rushing water. Anne could not bring herself to cross it, and waited instead at a belvedere, an overlook, just below the bridge. She waved when Paul reached the other end of the footbridge and turned to look for her. And an anxious dread churned up inside her until he was back by her side.

Paul stood close to her, as they leaned over the wooden railing of the belvedere. "I never tire of the sight of this torrent of water," he said.

"I've heard," Anne said "that in winter the mist freezes and forms an enormous cone of ice, like a sugar loaf, and people carry sleds up it to slide down. I would love to see these waters when they turn to ice."

He waited before answering her. Then he looked off in the distance and spoke in a more aloof, detached manner, as if musing to himself. "One day, the frozen falls saved my life." Then he brightened and smiled at her. "No, for me Montmorency is magnificent only when the falls run full and free."

They had returned to the carriage and were headed back toward her aunt's when Paul's manner changed, his voice becoming strained, his face tense.

"I must tell you…." He hesitated. Anne became alarmed when she realized he was struggling to speak. "I have a daughter. Emilie. She is three years old."

Anne was stunned. He was married. It had never entered her thoughts that he might be married.

Paul continued, his words stilted and forced. It had been over two years since he had seen Emilie. When his wife, who had always complained about the cold Canadian winters, had been introduced to the owner of sugar plantations in the Caribbean, she had divorced Paul, married the wealthier man, and now lived in the Virgin Islands. It would be years before Paul could afford a voyage to visit his little girl.

"I fear she may have forgotten who I am by now. Early one morning, last February, I took the train to Montmorency intent on throwing myself into the cataract. But it was covered with ice and I feared I might not die instantly. I am a coward, I did not want to freeze to death."

Anne's thoughts raced. Was this the person she had laughed with so easily a week ago. Married? No matter what he said, he was still married.

"How could it be?" Bewildered, she attempted to reorder her mind. "There is no divorce."

"I'm not Catholic."

Another blow. She was so naive. So foolish.

"But, you were at the Shrine. You attended Mass with me."

She had never considered that anyone in the church might not be Catholic. Anne knew what the nuns would say, that she was in an occasion of sin, that she must immediately ask Paul to stop the carriage and she should get out. But how could she do that? They were still way out in the country and she was not wearing proper shoes. But more than that, she did not want to leave Paul. When she finally spoke, her voice was almost a whisper.

"I am sorry, but I don't believe I can continue to see you."

He nodded. No further words passed between them on the trip back, the only sound the creak and rattle of the carriage and the muffled beat of the horse's hooves on the avenue.

When they reached Aunt Josie's, she turned to face him and was torn by the misery in his eyes. She searched desperately for an excuse to see him again.

"If it was your wife who left you, divorced you, then how can you be at fault?" He reached over, took her hand and held it for a moment, pressing it hard before he released it.

"I could not conceal this from you."

In the days that followed, Anne pondered this new development in her life. Never before had she had to make as serious a decision as this. And by herself, for she could not discuss it with Aunt Josie or Uncle Henri. Would she ever see Paul again? Might she? As the initial shock faded, she began to take a certain pleasure at her dilemma. She would share it with Louise.

August passed quickly. On the Saturday before she was to return to teaching, Anne visited the bookstore, wandering among the rows and displays, leafing through an occasional volume, all the time watching and waiting for a moment when there would be no customers within hearing, before she approached Paul.

"My aunt has invited you to dinner tomorrow to celebrate the start of my new teaching year. It would be lovely if you could drive me up to Beaupré afterwards."

She was surprised at her boldness. It had been Aunt Josie's suggestion, for Anne had still not told her about Paul's marriage, only that for personal reasons he had not been able to accept the previous invitation.

Paul accepted, his eyes quietly questioning Anne. She smiled briefly and left the bookstore.

After an early dinner, Paul and Anne walked the few blocks from *rue Ste. Geneviève* to the Terrace, the wide esplanade that looked out over the Lower Town and across the busy St. Lawrence River. The sunny promenade was thronged with clusters of families dressed in their Sunday best. A row of benches alongside the railing was mostly filled with old people dozing in the sunlight. Anne glimpsed Curé St. Armand, who occasionally said Mass at their school. She nodded respectfully but he did not seem to have seen her, apparently engrossed in a lively conversation with his companions.

Anne looked forward to the drive to Beaupré with mixed anticipation and dread. She felt occasional pangs of remorse about Aunt Josie, who seemed charmed by Paul, promising to drop by his bookstore during the week to look at newer authors. Neither Anne nor Paul spoke of what had passed between them on their return from the Falls at Montmorency. When there was a lull in the conversation, Anne quickly found another topic, avoiding what was foremost in her mind. But it was difficult.

Anne realized there was no decision to make, only rules to follow. Still, she would postpone what she knew was inevitable. Perhaps two, maybe three, more visits with Paul.

On the outskirts of Beaupré, Paul suddenly pulled the horse off the road and into a grove of trees and halted the carriage. She did not resist when he reached over and kissed her.

That night, before she fell asleep, she recaptured every detail of the day, dwelling again and again on the kiss.

The following day, after class was over, the students had all left. Anne was at her desk marking arithmetic papers when her concentration was broken by a fellow teacher who knocked as she opened the door, and, with urgency, said Anne must come quickly. Her uncle's carriage waited outside to bring her back to Quebec City. Word had been received from a priest down in New York that her mother was gravely ill. As the carriage raced down the Avenue Royale, Anne's mind filled with unspeakable fear.

In a frantic rush, Celeste packed their trunks, Uncle Henri embraced them goodbye, and the pair began their anxious journey down into the Hudson River Valley. During that long, tedious train ride, her aunt passed the time sharing memories of her sister. When Elise had expressed a wish to enter a cloister in Paris, their father was adamant. He would neither give his permission nor provide the expected dowry.

"My mother never mentioned wanting to be a nun," Anne protested.

"Elise accepted our father's decision. She never left the house and avoided social contacts outside the family. In a way, she turned our kitchen into her convent. She seemed content, even happy, singing as she scrubbed pots and chopped vegetables. I never expected her to marry.

"Then one day your father, the widowed brother of our laundress, accompanied by his two small sons, dropped off tablecloths his sister had brought home to iron. Understandably, he mistook your mother for a servant, for she was dressed in the plainest shift under a huge apron, and was peeling potatoes into a tub. They chatted a bit. Then he asked if he might accompany her to church on Sunday. We were delighted when she accepted. Any excuse to get her out of the kitchen.

"Later, when he proposed, she felt God had chosen her to care for his two little boys. My father was not pleased, but it seemed better than losing her forever behind the walls of a cloister. Little did he suspect your father would drag her far away, down to a mill town in Maine."

Her aunt paused and shook her head.

"I could not accept it. I begged. I pleaded with her. But she was adamant. She had made up her mind that God wanted her to marry Etienne Beauvois."

"And that is why my mother is poor while you are so wealthy?"

"In a way, *mon petit bijoux*, your mother is far richer than I. God gave her a lovely daughter."

Anne had heard only scraps of her parents' history. About the need to flee a failing farm in Quebec, and join the caravan of *Québécois* who reluctantly abandoned their farming heritage in exchange for jobs in mill towns along the rivers of Maine. She had never pictured her parents as being young, with lives separate from each other.

"I think it best that we pray," her aunt sighed.

The aunt and niece passed the rest of the journey quietly, whispering decade after decade of the rosary as they petitioned Our Lady to intercede for Elise Beauvois.

11

It was the last Wednesday in June. Anne had paused from trimming the tips off the green beans she had harvested earlier, in order to rest her aching wrist, when she discovered Liam's letter propped against the wall over the mantel.

Anne no longer watched for the postman. Her father collected whatever mail was delivered, with the unspoken expectation that Anne would attend, as her mother had before her, to whatever needed a response. The Haverstraw postmark was June 24th, the feast day of St. Jean Baptiste. It had sat there while she moved about the cabin, her mind numbed to everything but her daily tasks. Anne opened the envelope indifferently, with little interest in its contents.

As she read Liam's proposal of marriage her reaction was immediate. Never. The thought was outrageous. He was Catholic, but he was not French. He was a boy. That had become obvious to her last Christmas when he appeared on their doorstep full of bravado, his teeth chattering from the cold. What could have possessed him to suggest marriage? His audacity offended Anne. In an impulsive gesture, she was about to toss the paper into the fire, but, as the warmth of the low flames touched her hand, she stopped. She might need to refer to it when she composed her tactful refusal.

Why had she written to him in the first place? What could she have done to inspire such foolishness? This was a man on whom she hoped to practice, as she prepared herself to attract a suitable husband. She could never exchange sacred vows with Liam.

For a while, when she was younger, Anne had considered taking vows to become a nun. Attracted by the security, the freedom from any cares about her future. Everything settled, safe and secure, with Heaven guaranteed. The nuns had taught that religious life was holier than marriage. She could spend her life teaching children. She loved children.

Anne laughed bitterly. With her tarnished reputation, no convent would now open its doors to her. She examined the letter she was holding. Up in the right hand corner above the date, were the initials A.M.D.G. Her mother had marked every letter that way; "*ad majorem Dei gloriam* — to the greater glory of God." The Ursulines had taught Anne and her classmates to do likewise, urging them to begin every piece of work, every exam or composition, with this reminder that their work was dedicated to God.

That Liam should write it at the top of his letter confused her. Anne studied it again. Yes—A.M.D.G—and dated June 24th, a time of feasts and festivals. She doubted he knew how important that day is to French Canadians.

She placed Liam's letter back on the mantel, pondering how best to respond and, despite a wrist that ached from the effort, resumed topping and stringing the beans. Through the open window, she heard her father's voice, arguing. She knew he had no one there with him. All through her childhood, Anne had listened as her father sparred with invisible foes. It still alarmed her. In a moment, he might begin to bellow and smash his fists against the side of the cabin. His annoyance today seemed to be Lucien Lessard's team of strong horses that pulled his plow through the hard and rocky soil of this godforsaken valley.

Anne shuddered at the thought of her father's reaction to Louise's news. Of the disgrace of her having being seen alone in the company of a married man. Inevitably it would reach him. Come, perhaps, from a neighbor with a cousin visiting from Biddeford. Where could she hide?

"St. Anne. Good St. Anne, guide me," she pleaded.

As the ache from her wrist grew more intense, she abandoned the beans and crossed back to the fireplace, removed Liam's letter and brought it to the light of the window to read it once again.

She thought about his promotion to foreman. At the textile mill in Biddeford, it was well known that foremen earned their rank by demonstrating good judgment and maturity. Provided they were Irish, of course. She thought about how her mother decided to marry poor, illiterate Etienne Beauvois and raise his two motherless sons because she believed it was God's will.

She thought about the A.M.D.G. and June 24th.

Haverstraw might not be Quebec City, but it offered a life far from her father, and from this desolate farm. While she barely knew Liam, Anne was encouraged by the knowledge that he dedicated his marriage proposal to God, that he had the personal qualities of a foreman, and the distant but still pleasant memory of the laughter they shared that night they first met. He was no worse than her brothers, not that different from the men in Biddeford, except he was not French.

Anne pushed aside canning jars and baskets of beans to clear a place at the long table. Risking her father's disapproval, she lit the oil lamp and carried it to where she sat. Despite the pain of her wrist, she could hold a pen. In a brief note, at the top of which she printed A.M.D.G, Anne accepted Liam's proposal. Then walked back to the fireplace, tossed his letter onto the bed of embers, and watched while the paper blackened and curled.

12

An early September chill signaled that summer was on the wane. Liam was in high spirits as he and Ned climbed aboard the Albany local at West Haverstraw. He wore a second-hand suit he'd bought at Nathan's, a bright yellow bow tie, and a new straw boater. He carried his first pair of dress shoes in a sack, which he placed between them on the rattan seat. Ned's black suit was the same one he'd received the day he left the Order. After four years of Liz Farrelly's good cooking, it finally fit him.

"Not many people up and out so early on a Sunday morning. We might well have our own private railroad car, just like Andrew Carnegie," Liam chortled.

Ned had never been north of Haverstraw, preferring excursions down river. He was pleased to see that the clutter of buildings and people was quickly replaced by shrubs and rock face. The train ran close to the river, passed through a swampy lowlands and then entered a narrow passage through tall mountains that ran down to the water. It was breathtaking.

Above the river, a slit in the gray sea of clouds revealed a delicate pale pink sky that continued to emerge as he watched.

The previous afternoon, while he and Ned were waiting to have their hair cut, well-wishers drifted in and out of the barber shop, congratulating Liam, punching his upper arm, winking, nodding knowingly. Ned watched Liam closely, anticipating some sign of nervousness, some awareness that a major change in his life was about to take place. Liam seemed oblivious to anything more profound than deciding which tie to wear at the ceremony.

"Weren't they grand? All of them wishing me good luck, treating me like I was the King of England."

"They took you up to Diamond Street, I hear." Up the river to houses, called beauty shops, which were patronized by men from as far away as Albany and Schenectady. There were several of these houses along the river in Haverstraw, but Liam's friends avoided them. Diamond Street was different, a spectacle, worth the two-hour trip on the steamboat, so the word went around the tavern.

"Couldn't have it, they insisted. That I'd never been with a woman. Last chance, they said." He turned to Ned, waiting for his approval. "It was only a lark. It wasn't anything."

It didn't bother Ned. It was none of his business. Ned himself had visited brothels in Liverpool, after he'd left the Seminary. During those first few months, when he was drunk more often than sober. When he no longer knew who he was or what he believed or what purpose life held for him. When he was still hiding from the shame of a failed vocation.

"Does Anne know she'll be working at the boarding house?"

"Ah, no need to worry about Anne. She's a good sort."

"At least you'll have some privacy."

"Thanks to you. With no extra charge since she'll be helping Nora in the kitchen."

Ned wondered if the girl would mind the stale smell of fried cabbage and cigar smoke which clung to the walls and stairwells at Curran's. Soon the cold weather would set in, the windows and doors would be kept closed.

But this was foolishness, his thinking a farm girl, raised with cows and pigs, would be bothered by a smell or two. Hadn't he, in the seminary, soon got so he hardly noticed the rank body odors of over a hundred unbathed men?

At Liz Farrelly's, each morning the clean, cheerful smell of baking bread and brewed coffee seeped under the door into Ned's small back room.

They rode for a while, each in their own thoughts. Ned finally broke the silence.

"It still worries me, her thinking it was you that wrote the letters."

"And didn't I, now? Wasn't it me, after all, that told you what to say? Let it rest."

But Ned could not let it rest. He told himself over and over that it was out of his hands. Yet it continued to worry him. What particularly disturbed him was seeing A.M.D.G. at the top of her acceptance. If somehow she knew the true meaning of those letters, then he had grievously deceived a person whom he'd never even met.

But would she care? Would she laugh it off, as Liam did? Was she, perhaps, only imitating a pattern, design, rather than expressing faith? Suppose she didn't laugh?

In a small room off the sacristy of the church, Liam changed his shoes. Ned picked specks of lint off the shoulders and front of the second-hand jacket, then twisted and tucked Liam's bow tie into place. Liam's greatest concern seemed to be whether the rain would hold off so the party could be held on the lawn instead of in the barn.

Ned was stunned when he first caught sight of Anne standing at the door of the church. Who was this striking, auburn-haired woman? And where was Liam's bride? Where was the simpering little blond? Ned was torn by a sudden impulse to flee, to hide, and, at the same time, wanting to never take his eyes off this woman. He was steadied by a jab in his ribs. Liam took in Ned's astonishment with a triumphant smirk.

Throughout the ceremony Ned, with lowered eyes, fought to contain his composure, permitting himself only the briefest glance at Anne when the priest led the couple in their vows. Otherwise, he limited his gaze to the back of Liam's jacket.

Later, on the lawn outside the church, Liam introduced him to Anne: "Is she not a prize?" Cornered, Ned stiffened his resolve and looked directly at her.

"She is. That she is." Ned was in a terrible state, bewildered and confused by thoughts he ought not be thinking.

Ned's eyes briefly caught Anne's.

"At last. I meet one of Liam's mates. You must be a special friend, since he chose you to stand up for him."

Disconcerted by the hint of an accent that gave a musical quality to her voice, Ned was unable to respond. Finally, he blurted, "God bless you, Miss… Mrs. O'Connor." He quickly turned away from her, mortified at his clumsiness.

This instant and outrageous attraction he felt for Liam's new bride terrified Ned. How would he conquer it? Guard every thought, every word, every gesture, until this absurd fascination left him.

The rain held off and sunshine flooded the lawn of the church. An accordion player pumped out lively melodies while members of the Altar Society moved among the wedding guests, distributing lemonade and small pastries. Bottles of wine, sheltered from the sun, cooled in a tub beneath a weeping cherry tree. Ned observed that the maid of honor, Louise, while assisting the churchwomen, displayed so flirtatious a manner that even the oldest of the wives bristled and moved possessively toward their husbands.

Amid cheers and applause, the bride and groom were led over to an elaborately decorated cake. Helene Gaudet announced the cake had taken her three days of preparation. After the initial cut by Anne and Liam, followed by more clapping and hooting, Anne's father called for silence and summoned the couple to his side. The older man then reached over and grasped Liam's left hand, raising it high above his head.

"When we first met, I looked at his hands. I could see, these hands are not afraid of hard work."

He spoke a rapid patois. A handful of guests who spoke the same tongue, responded enthusiastically. The rest of the crowd smiled vaguely, not understanding, and waited. When they saw him draw from his inside coat pocket a long white envelope everyone began to murmur. With ceremony, the father handed the envelope to Liam. "Fifty acres of Lessard's finest land. Good, rich soil. A fine start for a hard worker. Later, Lessard might do business with you." The older man's eyes skimmed the crowd until they located Lucien Lessard, seated at an empty table at the far edge of the lawn and winked at him. Lessard nodded.

Trained only in classical French, Ned could not follow the older man's words. But, from gestures and inflections, he, along with everyone else, was convinced the white envelope contained a substantial gift, and he joined the claps and hollers of approval.

Ned looked first toward Liam who held a wine bottle aloft and smiled broadly at the cheering guests. Ned then darted a glance at Anne and could not read her expression. It seemed both wary and perplexed. Surprised that her father had not told her about what was in the envelope? When Ned looked again, she was smiling but it was a measured, detached smile. He forced his eyes away lest she turn and catch him studying her.

The accordion once again stirred the crowd into a lively jig. Louise, apparently giddy from wine, danced by herself in the midst of the revelers, tilting her shoulders and hips to the music. Ned came into her line of sight and she headed toward him.

"I'm curious, Liam's friend. You've had a frown on your face from the time the bride walked up the aisle. And you're standing here alongside the wedding cake as if to protect it from robbers while a young girl like me needs a dance partner." She lowered her ear until it touched her shoulder.

"I've got two left feet," he apologized. But Louise was not to be discouraged. She drew him onto the circle of lawn where most of the guests were twisting and bobbing. Ned circled his arm around the girl's waist as he listened for the beat his feet should attempt to match. It was a pleasantly disturbing moment for Ned. He had never danced with a woman before. Louise pushed and pulled him about and he found himself relaxed, even grinning.

"You're doing well," Louise assured him, speaking with a slight accent, similar to Anne's.

After Anne's trunk had been lifted onto the back of the train and the three were seated together, Liam's head dropped onto the front of his now-wrinkled suit and he began to snore. Anne was silent, tired no doubt from all the dancing and excitement of the day. Ned, relieved he did not have to make conversation, scanned the sky outside his window. The sun was about to drop behind a ridge of mountains to the west. It would be dark before they reached Haverstraw.

The woven cane backrest offered blessed relief as Anne pressed her shoulder blades against it, but the same shiny cane on the seat cushion allowed the fabric of her skirt to slide each time the railroad car twisted or lurched, so that she repeatedly found her hip pressing against Liam's, despite her effort to remain upright. The intimacy of the gesture, her body pressed against his, reminded her that soon she would be sharing her body with this man she had just married.

Helene and Yvette had teased her about "at last becoming a woman" and each had taken her aside and said they wished a friend had spoken to them ahead of time so it would not have been such a shock and, according to Yvette, such a disappointment. Helene sent away to Montgomery Ward for a fancy white cotton nightgown, which she presented to Anne at the train station. "I was afraid it wouldn't arrive in time and I'd have to mail it to you."

Anne had not been able to think of any questions to ask them, for her mind clouded over at any thought of the physical side of marriage. She had smiled and thanked them and quickly changed the subject.

It was so obviously central to the whole business of family, of children. Yet, at the same time, bewildering and shameful. Even now, Anne felt a blush begin to form at her throat. *Impure.* The word the nuns and priests used when they addressed the topic.

Impure thoughts—impure touch. Even Helene and Yvette giggled nervously when they alluded to the act of marriage. If they mentioned it, they spoke in lowered voices. And, certainly, never in the presence of their husbands.

And then there was that mysterious element of danger. Without specifying exactly what might take place, she and every other young woman she knew had been shepherded, guarded, protected, from the undesirable attentions of men.

Now that she was married, everything would be different. She would no longer have to worry about improper advances, or be concerned about what might be "impure." Would never again have to confess to a priest, as she had after she allowed Paul to kiss her.

She had chosen a church in the Lower Town, lest she be recognized.

"Touched you!" The confessor's growl had been edged with contempt. "What do you mean? Touched you?"

She'd stammered, "I let him kiss me."

"And," the elderly priest demanded, "are you affianced to this man?"

Anne dared not lie. "He is not a Catholic."

She flinched at his swift intake of breath. "You must agree to have nothing further to do with this man, or I will withhold absolution."

She agreed.

When she left the confessional, conscious that his booming voice had carried to the earshot of those outside waiting their turn, she lowered her eyes as she turned and approached the altar rail to repeat her penance.

No, she would never have to speak to a priest again about so personal and intimate a matter.

What would Liam expect of her? He was not demonstrative in any way. Had only kissed her the one time, at the wedding, when the priest told him to. So like her father. Anne had never seen her parents kiss or embrace. Whatever might have taken place between them physically evidently ceased at her birth, for her mother and she had shared the same bed from the time Anne was an infant. Her father and brothers slept in the other bedroom.

She and Liam would share a bed. Would he be different when it was only the two of them alone? Would he speak differently to her? More personally? Would he tell her that he loved her? Cared for her? Did she love Liam?

At that moment, Liam, half-asleep, burped and a sour smell of beer and vomit caused her to twist her face away.

Behind her, Ned heard the belch and observed Anne's reaction. He could no longer pretend that everything would turn out for the best. The fact was that this marriage had taken place and now this fine young woman sitting beside Liam, traveling toward Haverstraw, would climb the stairs to that attic, undress and....

No. He shook his head. No. He dare not think about such things.

What could have possessed her?

Ned struggled to untangle the bewildering events of the day. A sense of foreboding had clouded his thoughts since speaking with Anne's friend from Maine.

Louise, bubbling with happy memories of times she spent with Anne when they were children, spoke of picnics at Old Orchard Beach and of delivering dinner pails to their fathers at the textile mill.

Ned was concentrating on when and where he should move his feet and gave little attention to her chatter. Until he realized she was describing Anne's leaving Biddeford to attend school in Quebec.

"I missed her so, after she went to live with her aunt and uncle. She sent me several letters, at first, but I imagine her new friends and her studies kept her busy. When she'd come home for the New Year's blessing, we'd visit a bit, but she had changed and I felt our friendship was over. I was so glad when she began writing again after she'd finished school."

"Why did she leave her family? Why go to Quebec?"

"Her mother did not want her to work in the mill. Her aunt Josie lived in a beautiful house in Quebec City, with servants, and carriages." Delighted to have piqued Ned's interest, she continued, much as a proud parent might. "After she graduated from the convent, she taught school up there. Yes. Can you imagine? She was a teacher."

Ned's eyes must have reflected his dismay, for a sudden look of horror crossed Louise's face. "*Mon Dieu*, I cannot not drink wine. Anne made me promise never to tell."

Ned thought back to the moment before the vows were recited, when the priest had announced the ritual admonition, "If anyone knows of a reason…" and Ned had wanted to raise his hand. But what could he say? She thinks he can read and write but he cannot. And he's not a foreman. Ned would have been laughed at. He could imagine the gasps that would have scattered throughout the church, see the priest's angry face, watch the ushers rise to remove him so the ceremony could proceed.

Louise confirmed Ned's worst fears. He had constructed a shameful deception. Ned winced as he remembered embellishing Liam's thoughts, here and there tacking on a comment of his own. He'd been fascinated. Fascinated to be exchanging letters with a girl. A girl who was hardly more than paper and ink. Gradually over the months, as the letters flowed back and forth, Ned had begun to pretend that she was really writing to him.

His suspicion that envy might have fueled his concern about the marriage, as well as the threat of ridicule, silenced him.

To salve his guilt, he'd recited prayers asking God to guide Liam and Anne, but found no comfort, recognizing a pathetic attempt to turn over to God what was his own responsibility. Wasn't he the fine one to be saying prayers? What did he know, anymore, of God, or of anything else, for that matter?

Louise had pleaded with him to forget everything she'd said about Quebec. He'd wanted to ask her more about Anne, but was acutely aware of inquiring looks from the other guests. He gave his word. He could not figure out why Anne wanted to keep such an accomplishment a secret. And, how she could settle for someone like Liam O'Connor? He was not evil or bad, but he was immature and crude. His only interest in life was the pursuit of wealth. Ned felt that Liam would plow through anything or anyone who threatened his dream.

Liam had debts to settle back in Ireland. With his uncle's wife, Sarah, who had robbed him and his mother of the family farm in Connamara.

Liam had heard Sarah, her eyebrows arched in solicitous bewilderment, question his newly widowed mother. "How will you ever manage?" she'd asked. "What will you do?" And, when the numbed woman failed to respond, Sarah began to weave her treacherous plan. "You would not expect my husband to continue to work your farm as well as his own. Which he's been glad to do for the moment, in memory of his brother, God rest his soul. But only for the while, you understand."

Hardly a month had passed before Sarah was back to their cottage with a letter from New York, from her nephew, Father Frank, whose parish was in a place called Hell's Kitchen. She waved it excitedly. Sarah could read, for she had attended school in Dublin. Her nephew, as she'd suspected, needed a housekeeper, for the old woman who cooked for him was failing rapidly.

Liam's mother, frantic with grief and worry, never questioned the shabby bargain. The desperate widow signed over her husband's land for the price of passage to America, where, as Sarah assured her, "God has important work for you to do." After five miserable weeks in the stinking hold of a ship, she discovered that the priest had no intention of turning out the old housekeeper. In fact, Liam's mother would have to share the old woman's bed. And furthermore, that Sarah had not mentioned any son. Sarah's plan was for Liam to remain in Connamara, and continue to work the farm, which Liam agreed, even begged to do. The farm was the only life he'd ever known. But his mother knew Sarah would not treat him well, and, besides, she could not bear to leave him behind. She'd dressed him in his dead father's clothes and dragged him with her to America.

The priest, dismayed, had no room for a strapping lad like Liam who, though only thirteen, had outgrown his father's suit. The threadbare cloth covered neither his wrists nor his ankles. His father's heavy brogues pinched toes accustomed to the freedom and feel of cool earth. Liam knew instantly, from the priest's hesitant greeting, that he was in trouble.

After the simmering disappointment and anger that had stewed inside him for five weeks on that filthy ship, Liam now vowed that he would become wealthy.

"For isn't it money that makes all the difference? Between the one who gives the orders and the one who has to take them." He pledged, as well, that one day he'd bring a pot of money back to Ireland. And buy back not only his father's farm but his uncle's as well, and he'd spread the word throughout the hills of Connamara of the treacherous Sarah.

The following winter, Liam had cajoled a nun at the orphanage into letting him join the older boys and traipse the nine miles up to Rockland Lake where the Knickerbocker Ice Company was cutting ice, where he earned his first bit of money. It was there, at Rockland Lake, working alongside the furloughed brick workers, that he first heard of Haverstraw, and its brickyards and boarding houses. As soon as the word spread that he was from Connamara, Liam was assured a job in Curran's brickyard.

"Watch for when the river opens up and the barges can get through the ice. Then bring yourself up to Farrelly's tavern on Broad Street. We'll fix you up fine."

No, Ned admitted to himself, Liam was not a bad man. A hard worker, he pulled his own weight. Got along well with others. But he was no proper husband for this young woman.

What could have possessed her to marry him? How would she bear the filth and noise of Curran's boarding house? Liam had gleefully confided to Ned that his marriage would not to make a dent in his bank account. Nora Ferguson had agreed that Anne's help in the kitchen would cover the additional cost of her board.

The boarding house on Allison Street was the former home of Vincent Curran, owner of the brickyard. As his fortunes had grown, so had his wife's notions regarding social appearances. These notions eventually led him to abandon a perfectly good two-story frame house, in which he had installed an indoor bathroom in a vain attempt to placate his wife. He followed the example of other successful neighbors who had built larger, grander homes up on Hudson Avenue, on the side of the mountain in Upper Haverstraw, where from their bedroom windows they could watch the sun come up over the Hudson. Curran kept the original home and installed the capable widow, Nora Ferguson, to run it as a boarding house for his workers. Ned had stayed there when he first arrived in Haverstraw. Beds were crammed into all four rooms on the second floor, often requiring an occupant to climb back and forth over another man's mattress to reach the slop pail in the hall, thus adding to the roars and oaths which filled the house much of the time the men were there.

Liam was reluctant to move from a place where his board and lodgings were currently included in his pay. Ned could not calculate Liam's thinking — that this marriage was to increase his fortunes rather than place a drain on them. He had hounded Liam, insisting a new bride could not be expected to share a room with strangers on the other side of a canvas drape. The attic had been Nora Ferguson's suggestion, after Liam explained his predicament.

Two days before the wedding, Ned, Liam, and Mrs. Ferguson had climbed the narrow attic stairs and, while the two men cleared a space among the clutter of boxes and discarded furniture, she selected the best of an assortment of old mattresses propped against the sloping rafters and together, crouching and tugging, and occasionally cracking their skulls against a wooden beam, they stacked three in a newly cleared area.

"I'll find you a nice, clean chamber pot," Nora promised.

As the train curved southward, Ned could see ahead the towers of the military academy at West Point, and, to his left, the leaden surface of the Hudson. The river had only a scattering of Sunday traffic, a string of empty brick barges being towed further upriver, a handful of skiffs and rowboats slowly threading the surface, their bobbing lanterns glowing dimly. Overhead, above the treetops, twilight drained from the sky. The rain was holding.

Ned heard Liam groan when a sudden jolting of the train briefly roused him. Ned turned and saw Liam slowly stretch his body, thrusting forth his chest, elbows braced, and shook his tousled curls. The lapels of his suit were crumpled and the bow tie twisted a quarter turn from his chin. He moaned again, belched and a whiff of stale beer carried across the aisle.

Ned turned back to the river and watched through the window the flickering lanterns, which pierced the descending dusk. His mind churned with the doubts and confusion of the day. Despite his fatigue, he was reluctant that the train ride end for he saw no future for this marriage other than one of trouble and pain. Ned heard the sound of paper being torn, watched him pull something from an envelope, then, Liam's voice, slurred and thick.

"Umph! No money. Letter."

Ah, thought Ned, Liam will need assistance with this. It could be the deception's undoing, when he turned to his new wife, either sheepish or filled with bravado, to show her her father's letter and acknowledge he could not read it. The sooner the better. Instead, he suspected Liam would bring the envelope to the tavern for him to decipher.

The train continued to sway and jolt, and Ned longed to be back in his little room on Broad Street, amid the reassuring scents of Liz Farrelly's well-ordered home.

13

They decided to leave her trunk in the kitchen until morning. The commingled smell of boiled cabbage, stale tobacco, and human odors stunned Anne and she resorted to breathing through her mouth, a habit she had mastered on the farm when her chores took her past the dung heap.

From the dim light of the lantern she carried, Anne saw, under the rafters, a pile of mattresses on the floor. She stifled a gasp and cautioned herself that in Chestnut Grove she'd slept in a loft, although there she had a cot. Surely, this was only a temporary arrangement until proper accommodations could be found. The air up here in the attic, though dusty, was fresher than below, sealed off by a door at the foot of its narrow flight of stairs.

"Watch your head, watch your head," Liam mumbled, warning of the low-hanging beams. Stooping as she moved around in the semi-darkness, her foot struck something, followed by the clatter of metal on the wood floor. She groped around at her feet and recognized a faint smell of urine and knew she had knocked the lid off an empty slop pail.

Liam threw himself, fully dressed, onto the mattresses, not bothering to pull a blanket over him. By the time she had removed her blue serge traveling suit and her corset, and had slipped out of her cambric drawers, so that she was wearing only a muslin slip, he was snoring.

She felt both rejection and relief. Anne had been curious, uncertain how she would react to the intimacies she knew were expected of a wife. Liam never mentioned love. Anne was not comfortable saying it herself. Do I love him? She felt a certain gratitude for his role in helping her escape the tedious world of the farm and the threat of Lessard. Freed from her father's dictates and tantrums.

She would make him a good wife. She would work hard, do her part, and carry her share. Still, when she honestly examined her expectations, it seemed she was mentally holding her breath, until something better happened.

The next morning, shocked from sleep by the predawn whistles of the brickyards, she heard Liam scramble into his clothes and hurry down the stairs. She fell back to sleep, until a ray of sunlight, shining through a small grime-coated window, roused her.

Anne looked up at the old timbers overhead, and over at the narrow staircase and wondered about fire. In her father's hearth, the driest wood burned quickest. Last night Mrs. Ferguson had cautioned that she did not permit oil lamps above the first floor, only stubs of candles secured in metal lanterns.

After twice painfully cracking her head against the rafters, she remembered to crouch while she dressed and to stand erect only in the center of the attic.

Anne, in her traveling suit, followed the smell of coffee and then the glow of light until she found Nora Ferguson standing before a stove. Her fat hands were clasped around a long wooden stick with which she slowly stirred the contents of a large black pot. Looking up from her efforts, she noticed Anne, greeted her with a cheerful "Morning," and returned to her stirring.

"I'll be ready for work as soon as I can change my clothes," Anne replied.

She found the trunk just inside the back door where Liam and Ned had left it. The last item she had packed, the pale blue satin dress, which she had worn at the wedding, lay on top and, as she lifted it out, it seemed to her that years had passed since she last wore it and a lifetime since Aunt Josie's seamstress first delivered it to her. Anne brought it into the center of the kitchen under the light of the large kerosene lamp and began to examine it for stains and damage.

"Have to keep stirring the oats so they don't burn," Nora Ferguson explained with a laugh, looking over her shoulder to see what Anne was up to. As she turned away from the stove, she dropped the stick so that it fell back into the pot, propped against the rim. She came closer, her eyes widening as she took in the shimmering satin, the embroidered flowers stitched on the bodice and across the skirt. She turned a wondering gaze back to Anne, sweeping it over her, up, down, and up again. "Well, now," the older woman murmured as she returned to the stove.

Anne dug further down into the trunk and found a change of underclothes and the heavy brown shoes she had carefully cleaned and polished.

Nora Ferguson was silent for a moment, then said emphatically, "Your trunk can stay in my room. That attic...it's no place for such a dress. And you can wash and change down here as well."

Nora Ferguson led her through a small room in which an unmade bed occupied most of the space and showed her the adjoining room, which contained a water closet, a pedestaled wash basin and a gleaming white bathtub.

"It's my good luck that the owner put this in, hoping to satisfy his wife. And not have to build her a grander home up the mountain."

"Thank you, Mrs. Ferguson," Anne said gratefully, her heart lifting. She had not allowed herself to dwell on the privations of the room upstairs, but this kind gesture by Mrs. Ferguson reassured her that things were already looking better. "Liam said I'll be helping you in the kitchen. What can I do?"

14

Each day, the dining room floor needed to be swept. The cracked linoleum was scattered with remnants of the previous meal, as well as dirt carried in on the men's clothing. As usual, today Anne made a pile of the rubbish, collecting the mess onto a dustpan, and dumped it into a barrel outside the kitchen door. The glass chimneys of the large oil lamp that hung over the dining room table were gray with soot. She placed the soiled glass on the scarred table top, went in search of scissors to trim the wicks and found a wire chimney brush hanging on a nail in the broom closet, identical to one Celeste, Aunt Josie's housekeeper, had taught her to use.

As Anne struggled to rotate the brush, she looked with disgust at the cigar ashes that littered the table. The card players. They were an obnoxious bunch. Their shouts and oaths, as well as their cigar smoke, drifted up the stairs and into the attic, in spite of the closed door.

Liam never joined the card game after supper. Instead, he'd slip out to Farrelly's for a pint and to visit with his mates. When he returned, Anne would be finishing up her chores. After an exchange of wisecracks with the card players, he'd come to the kitchen and lean impatiently against the doorframe until she put down her work and accompanied him upstairs. The card players listened for their footsteps and never failed to call out suggestions and advice. Liam usually chuckled but Anne's cheeks burned.

Their second night together, Anne had worn the white night-gown Yvette had given her as a wedding gift. In the candle-lit attic, Liam may not have noticed. He pulled it up, quickly attended to his needs, then turned away from her and fell asleep. The nervous anticipation that proceeded her initiation into marriage left her.

The noisy card players did not bother Liam. From the moment he laid his head on the pillow, nothing woke him until the whistle blew at four o'clock the next morning. That blast propelled him out of bed, into his clothes and down the stairs, in a race to be first man onto the yard. A sort of game the workers played.

First, that is, after Charlie Stone. Because Anne did not sleep well, she learned to listen for the creak of Charlie's bicycle, as he pedaled his way through the dark streets and down into the yard to the paymaster's office, the soft clang of his lantern banging against the frame of his bicycle. Minutes later, whistles pierced the quiet of predawn with a bedlam of sound. Every yard had its own unique wail.

Nora Ferguson said no one complained about the racket. "It's part of Haverstraw. Bricks are our gold. They build the fine houses and pay the butcher and the baker. As well as all the boarding houses and saloons, stables and sawmills. It's bricks that built three hotels, the library, and all the churches. Paid to bring water down from Cedar Pond, gas lines to light our homes. And the banks, of course. We have almost as many banks as churches."

So Anne changed her mind about the whistles. She compared them to roosters. On the farm, one would crow and another answer and then another, in a sort of singsong that, after a while, made her laugh. That was one thing she shared with her father, their delight at the crowing of the cocks.

Anne found Nora an agreeable boss and, after a day or two,

she began to feel useful. Meals were the major work. Preparation and clean up. Which left several free hours in the middle of the day.

"Go take a walk around the village," Nora urged. "Find out for yourself why Haverstraw is famous."

Anne discovered the King's Daughters Library just down the road from the boarding house. Hundreds of books. Electric chandeliers. An enormous window in the upstairs room, with tables and chairs. At last. A place to read, to write letters. The clean, quiet, orderly building put Anne in mind of a convent.

"Come, Miss," Nora Ferguson called from the kitchen, interrupting her reverie. "The breakfast whistle is about to sound, the pails are ready. You'll bring them down today. Hurry now. The men carry on something fierce if their oats are cold. You'll need heavy boots for the mud; get some from the bottom cupboard near the back door."

Anne returned to the kitchen carrying the lamp chimneys and found eight long-handled pails lined up on the drainboard of the sink. She placed the blackened glass back on the dining room table. When she returned from delivering the breakfasts she'd finish cleaning them.

Anne joined a procession of women and children carrying meal pails down the hillside toward where the brickyards bordered the river. In front of her was a treeless, desolate scene, its only colors shades of gray. Even the river was slate. The embankment she descended had been carved into a massive staircase of broad steps dotted with men and horse carts. At the foot of the steps, where the ground spread level, lay long rows of raw bricks, and, past them, open sheds with clusters of men moving about, shouting at each other. Beyond, smoke poured from enormously tall chimneys. Even further out, close to the river's edge, a row of shanties.

She thought back to her childhood in Biddeford, where she often brought her father his dinner at the textile mill. She had to find her way through a warren of dark alleys until she reached the doorway leading to the dye room, down in the bowels of the mill where, in the winter, the dank air that settled into her hair froze against her forehead as she hurried back home.

To reach Curran's brickyard, she had to cross a small stream. The wet clay bottom sucked at her boots and threatened her balance. The warmth of the pails knocking against her thighs, brought back memories of Chestnut Grove. Of buckets filled with foaming milk, the steam rising from them into the morning chill.

Ned Walsh appeared in front of her, heading out of Curran's yard. As he drew closer and recognized her, an astonished, perplexed frown creased his face.

"And what would you be doing here, Miss...Mrs.?"

"Nora Ferguson told me to bring down the breakfasts."

"Give them here." He had grabbed the handles of the pails before she realized what he was up to. "This is no work for you," he muttered brusquely, and turned back toward the brickyard. Anne watched him disappear behind a long, wooden shed. What could Ned mean by "this is no work for you?" She was prepared to do her part. Why should she not deliver the food?

Ned confused her. Curt and distant one moment, considerate of her the next. Two days ago, she came upon him in the library. He had simply nodded and turned back to scan the book stacks, then abruptly, and without any further word, left. He was a puzzle. So strange at the wedding. Not speaking one word to her during the long train ride to Haverstraw. Did he not approve of her as a wife for Liam? Had he realized how much older she was? Yet, Ned Walsh's kindness—for that's what it was—kindness, struck her. He had just expressed concern for her and, for the first time since she'd left Canada, she felt less alone. She suspected what Ned wanted to protect her from. While serving dinner, hands pinched and fondled her body as she carried heavy platters of food. The first time she had shrieked in dismay. Liam roared with laughter, along with the others.

Anne enjoyed a moment of solitude as she slowly climbed the clay embankment back to the boarding house. She thought back to that Easter afternoon when, climbing a different hillside, she discovered she no longer feared her father and could leave his farm.

Anne felt no closer to Liam than she had the day of her wedding. He made no effort to draw her into his world. She was to be shown off as some sort of prize. Yesterday, he had her put on her dark blue traveling suit and her mother's hat and accompany him to the bank where he introduced her to Mr. Curran. The banker gave them barely a glance and a nod.

The marriage was a fair trade. He used her to impress people, while she'd used him to escape from her father. She could put up with the boarding house arrangement, and the card players, for a while. After the brickyards shut down for the winter, they would return to Chestnut Grove. Maybe not until spring, when the land was ready for planting. By then she should be with child, and once it was born nothing else would matter.

She had mixed feelings about her father's gift. While it offered them a start in life, the less desirable part was having to live with her father until they found a home of their own. It was clear to Anne that, by providing the land, her father was investing in Liam's broad back and callused hands as well in as a housekeeper.

But she was not certain about leaving Haverstraw. She liked the library, the shops, the general bustle of activity. Haverstraw was wonderful. Three hotels, an opera house, a theater where James M. Cohan had appeared. A railroad passing through, up to Canada and down into New Jersey. A person could be in New York City in less than two hours.

Anne removed her mud-caked boots and left them at the foot of the back stoop, then retrieved her shoes. She found a dull knife and a scrub brush and was about to clean the boots when

Nora Ferguson appeared in the kitchen, holding a large bundle of sheets in her arms.

"When you're finished there, I want you to drop these off at the laundry on Center Street and pick up last week's order. Take one of the wagons out back. Be sure it's a clean one. Not the one your husband uses to slop his hog." Liam kept a pig down on the clay bank which he fed with hotel garbage.

Nora jammed the soiled linens into two cotton sacks. She tied the drawstrings at the top of each and propped them against the kitchen wall.

"I see you're working on the lamps. There are scissors in the pantry drawer to trim them, and," pointing, "a tin of lamp oil in that cabinet." Nora's voice was rough and her manner direct, but she showed neither resentment nor impatience as she instructed Anne. "And, before you go, hang these blankets out back to get some of the camphor stink out of them. The cold weather will be here soon." She gestured toward a pile of folded blankets.

While Anne stretched the wool blankets over the clotheslines in the patch of ground behind the boarding house, she discovered she had a fine view from there of the river. Framed between two clumps of lilacs, with no chimneys or sheds to obstruct the vista, it seemed calm, placid. She knew that strong currents flowed beneath the fishing boats and tug-drawn barges, the sloops and schooners and small skiffs that dotted its slate gray surface. Ships depended on those tides to carry them up and down its broad channel.

She stole an extra moment to study the river, then hurried back toward the kitchen. She stumbled and looking down saw that the hard packed soil was broken into crevices of differing widths and depths, one of them as wide as her foot. She was familiar with soil that had been ploughed, but what she saw at her feet seemed more a preparation for planting without having first overturned the dirt. Ready for seeds, or even potatoes to be dropped into the deeper crevices, and with small effort, covered over. She looked around the weed-filled yard, at overgrown flower beds and untended fruit trees. Were she not leaving in five or six months, she would try to restore this neglected garden.

In Chestnut Grove, she would plant flowers, as well as a kitchen garden. Her father intended them to share his small cabin. That would only be at first. There had to be an abandoned barn or shed she and Liam could make livable. Any place away from her father.

15

L ater that afternoon, Ned looked up from the bar and watched Liam approach. In a friendly voice he asked, "How's our new-lywed friend today?"

The grin was not returned. Instead, Liam replied with a testi-ness Ned had never heard from him. "You brought the break-fasts down this morning."

"Of course, I did. Fortunately, I came across Anne stumbling through that muck."

"I wanted the men to see her. To see what I've got."

"She's not a prize mare to be shown off."

"She's a thoroughbred. She's that."

Ned stared at Liam, dumbfounded. Was there any talking to the man?

Ned silently vowed that tomorrow morning, and every morn-ing, he'd be ready when Anne came by with the pails.

Ned attempted to change the subject. "What would you say to this Sunday, we climb the Tor with Anne? We can show her the river. How about that?"

Still miffed, Liam shrugged. "Maybe. We'll see. But I've more pressing business today, finding the money for McCauley's schoo-ner. I hate to touch my savings. I'm considering selling that prop-erty Anne's father gave me."

Ned was astounded, then chagrined that he allowed this fellow to upset him so.

"Gave you? He gave to both of you. Has Anne agreed?"

"It was given like a dowry. To do with as I choose."

"How much do you hope to gain from it?"

"Well, I need fifteen hundred, to match what Mr. Curran will loan me."

Ned rubbed his palm over his face and exhaled. He made a quick calculation of his finances, trusting he might borrow the rest from Liz.

"Fifteen hundred dollars? You might have a buyer, Liam."

"From you? What would you do with a farm up in the country?"

"It's time for me to leave here. I prefer the country to the commotion of city life."

Delighted at the possibility of having raised the cash, Liam was restored to his usual good humor. When Ned reintroduced the idea of a climb of the Tor on Sunday, Liam enthusiastically agreed.

The crisp October day was a perfect one for climbing the Tor. It was filled with sunlight and hardly a wind until the peak, where mild, cooling gusts tempered the intensity of the sun. Gasping for breath, the trio reached the summit, where they rested briefly to regain energy. Then they stood with their hands as shields for their eyes and silently studied the scene that lay before them.

Anne gazed at the ribbon of river that twisted from a slender cut in the north to widen at her feet, then narrow slightly and curve out of sight, behind jutting southern palisades.

"The Hudson River. An amazing sight," Anne exclaimed, as she tucked wayward strands of hair back behind her ears.

"That's Haverstraw Bay out there," Ned told her. "The widest part of the Hudson, three miles across."

"Schoolmaster, are we to have a lesson today?" Liam asked, a trace of annoyance in his voice.

Anne, embarrassed for Ned, said, "I enjoy learning about such things."

"Then stick around the schoolmaster. You'll hear more than you'd ever want to know."

Anne was tempted to defend Ned, but suspected her husband had responded to something other than Ned's remark. Her brothers had often bantered with each other, chosing words instead of fists. But this day was too pleasant to be spent in male jousting. She turned back to the captivating sight that lay at her feet.

On the far side the river, the sun glinted off the windows of a train snaking its way north along the eastern shoreline. She raised her eyes slightly and saw, beyond the railroad track, wave upon wave of rounded hills, in shades of deep blues and lavender that stretched into the distance. Immediately below her, trees hid much of the village that lay at the base of the mountain. The wasteland of clay banks and mud holes were concealed as well, with only an occasional chimney to mark the engine house of a brickyard. The collection of drying sheds, their long, narrow roofs stretching shabby black fingers over the desolate clay fields toward the river, were lost beneath the branches.

Her gaze traveled again to the hills beyond the river. How many days of walking would it take to reach beyond the limit of her sight? She turned away to look northward, where already the changing leaves of autumn flecked the green coverlet with gold and orange. Somewhere, hidden up among those trees, lay her father's farm. She wondered whether the Lessard girl had served him his dinner by now. Had she twisted the neck off a chicken and roasted it in the heavy black pot, as Anne had shown her? Was everything working out up there?

She thought it best not to share these thoughts with her new husband. Better to wait and see how Liam and her father got along and what sort of farmer he made. Certainly, as her father had pointed out, Liam was not afraid of hard work.

Anne turned back to the river. As she gazed on the broad expanse of quiet, sun-dappled water, she found it difficult to shift her eyes away. The river drew her from the mountain with a warm, enveloping welcome. It was as if she'd entered it, become part of it. The men's chatter receded and their voices seemed far away.

Maybe, if Paul were beside her instead of Liam, she would tell him how the river called to her.

Ned's voice brought her back up the mountain.

"There," he gestured "lies Albany, Kingston, West Point. Perhaps you'd like to visit the Point. Would you like that, Mrs. O'Connor?... Anne? What about it, Liam?"

She had asked Ned to call her Anne and he agreed he would. Why did he find it so difficult?

Ned pointed in the general direction of her father's farm. Anne waited for Liam to respond, but he gave no indiction he heard Ned. Standing on a rocky shelf which jutted out from the summit, hands on his hips, his head was bent forward as he peered southward.

Anne remembered a sunlit Sunday in Canada when Paul had stood like that, the day when he had brought her to the Falls at Montmorency. Together, they had leaned over a waist-high metal fence and watched the tumbling yellow waters cascade onto rocks below, releasing plumes of white spray filled with rainbows, before the turbulence was swallowed into quiet eddies that eased southward into the St. Lawrence River.

Above them, people were crossing a footbridge over the Falls.

"Come," Paul said, "the view from up there is marvelous."

"No. The height makes me cringe. You go on while I wait here."

A little further up the path, Paul found an overlook, a belvedere, where she could feel safe, and he continued up to the footbridge. When, finally, she was able to identify him among the others out on the bridge, she waved and he returned her signal.

Anne stepped out onto the rocky shelf and stood next to Liam. Sensing her presence without turning, he placed an arm around her shoulders and pulled her possessively close. It felt protective and exciting at the same time. Other than the night when they had danced, Liam never held her.

With his other arm, Liam pointed southward. "Down there about six miles, past that first row of hills, is Rockland Lake. I was fourteen when I earned my first wages. At the Knickerbocker Ice Company. I worked in the big sheds. I packed sawdust around the blocks of ice. This winter after the Hudson freezes and the barges can't get through, we'll all be down there. Ice cutting is a good match for us. The brickyards lay us off until the spring, when the river breaks up and the brick barges can get through. The pay isn't much but everyone's glad to get the money. Only an hour's walk alongside the river. Some of the men ice skate each way."

Ned added, "It's a picture. The blue sky. Horses plowing the snow away so the ice underneath doesn't melt and horses dragging long saws to mark the blocks. Men hunched over hand saws carving the blocks loose."

"Ned wastes his time on things no one else would bother to notice," Liam commented. "It's bloody hard work, that's what it is." He gave Ned a poke with his elbow that unbalanced the slighter man who had to struggle to maintain his footing.

Impulsively, Anne quickly reached out her hand out to steady him, but, just as impulsively, drew it back.

"Are you trying to kill me?" Ned asked playfully.

Anne calculated Liam's age. "Fourteen? You've been a brick worker since you were fourteen?"

"Almost fifteen. The mates in the ice shed heard me curse in Irish and discovered I was from Connamara. They guaranteed me a job in the brickyard come spring. 'When the river ice breaks up,' they said, 'and you see boats moving about, come up to

Haverstraw.' This is my fifth year at Curran's."

"You left school at fourteen?" It began to dawn on Anne how little she knew about Liam. If he was fourteen, five years ago, then he was only nineteen. She had married a nineteen-year-old boy.

"Yep, I was finished with school," he muttered with a scowl.

The words had a sullen note so she quickly changed the topic. "I imagine you've both visited Manhattan."

Her question transformed Liam. As if a pump had been primed, the words poured out from him.

"Manhattan. No place like it. Horns, whistles, bells, and voices yelling, newsboys shrieking. Hooves clattering, wagon wheels rattling over the cobblestones. And the smell of the place. It stinks. Piles of steaming dung everywhere. Street cleaners with brooms and shovels battle the pigs for it. And dogs. Yelping, barking dogs. Above the street there's a railroad and showers of sparks fall down on you when a train passes over. New York is the greatest place on earth." Liam's feet shuffled and danced as he spoke, his eyes glowed.

He gulped a deep breath and continued.

"One morning, the barge left me at the 51st Street pier and I was headed for Curley's saloon, when a loaded brewery wagon turned a corner in front of me and tipped over. Barrels of ale rolled every which way. A couple of them smashed and the ale foamed out over the cobblestones. Men came from of nowhere, like a pack of rats, their hats held out to scoop up the ale. All of them roaring with laughter. The horses struggling to stand, churning their hooves. It was pitiful. I roared at the sight of it."

He choked with laughter as he recreated the scene. Liam held his hands in front of him, as if he held an enormous basket filled with treasure.

"And people—gobs of people. The place is alive with people. Some streets are so thick with people you can't see the pavement. Pushing and shoving past rows of wagons heaped with cabbages and apples and bread. Buildings! Block after block after block of them, brick buildings as far as you can see. "

His voice trailed off, his eyes shining.

Anne glanced over at Ned. His eyes had an unfocused, brooding quality, his head nodding slightly. Both men lost in their thoughts.

Liam's passionate outburst surprised Anne. His letters had never mentioned New York City. He wrote of floating down the Hudson on a brick barge where his job was splashing river water on the outside row of pale bricks to darken them the red color of more costly prime bricks.

Her thoughts brightened. There were still things to discover about Liam. A.M.D.G.? He did not attend church. Each Sunday, he was up at the lakes, chopping down trees for the brick furnaces.

There would be time to learn of each other when they moved to Chestnut Grove where they would spend more time together. But—he was only nineteen?

16

The kitchen was filled with appetizing aromas. Beef stew, the men's favorite meal. Over at the stove, Nora browned chunks of meat in a large iron skillet, while Anne scrapped carrot parings into the sink.

She turned toward the older woman and pointed a paring knife toward the ceiling. "I have to find a warmer place to sleep than that attic. The wind off the river blows straight through the roof. When I get out of bed, the floor is like ice beneath my feet."

Nora grunted. "I've wondered how long you'd put up with that garret."

"I want a place to cook, and enough room for a bed, a chair and a lamp. Only for a few months, until we move next spring."

"You're leaving? I haven't heard Liam talk about leaving."

"You know Liam. Never has much to say. When I ask him a question, he's always too busy to listen. Up and out of here at the crack of dawn; and half-asleep by the time I've finished my work down here. Sundays, off to Lake Welch with the loggers before I'm back from church.

"Yes," Nora agreed, "he certainly has his way when he wants to avoid me. He tracks clay all through the place, no matter how often I tell him the rule is no work boots above the cellar. 'Oh, Nora,' he'll say, 'my mind was elsewhere. I have such a terrible lot to think about.'" She shrugged her shoulders and shook her head.

"At our wedding," Anne explained, "my father gave us fifty acres of land. His scheme, I know, is to get the two of us back with him. To have Liam help with the plowing while I cook his dinner or scrub his filthy overalls. We'll have to stay with him at first, but I'll find some sort of shed where we can live while we're building our own place. I'll be expecting our first child by then, so we'll have to have it snug and warm before the winter arrives. I hate to leave Haverstraw. Above all, leaving you. You've been so kind. Letting me use your bathroom and all. It's been wonderful having someone I can talk to."

"Kind, am I? Ha! If that gets around, the men will trample me underfoot." Nora added another batch of beef to the skillet.

"Well," Nora said, "you probably won't be the only ones to leave. Come spring, when the yards reopen, the men will be back on the clay banks, digging closer and closer to the houses. Hardly a day goes by that I don't hear of another crack in the ground. Mamie Finnigan says that yesterday morning when she put the ashes out, there was a split in the road half the length of Liberty Street. It had closed back up by sundown. Word's going round that when the worst of the winter is past, but before the ground softens, Curran intends to find us all another place. Plans to pick this house up and move it to an empty lot on Division Street. Thinks the clay underneath us will more than justify the expense."

Nora emptied another skillet of browned beef into a large pot that simmered on the stove. She tossed chopped onions into the drippings and in no time the skillet gave off the tantalizing smell of caramelizing onions. Anne brought over the carrots and added them to the pot.

"Doesn't Curran have other accomodations for his workers?"

"He does, indeed. All over Haverstraw. It's said that Curran has bought up half the village. There are plenty of places, if your man wasn't so tight with his pennies. You've seen the shanties down on the clay pit. They're not fancy, but you'd have a stove and peace and quiet at night. Of course, the ground is pocked with mud holes so you'd have to watch your step when you use the privy. Pump your own water."

Anne wrinkled her nose. She'd passed by one the day she carried the meal pails. A pig had run out the door and she had shuddered, imagining the stink inside. The clay bank was littered with chunks of broken bricks and abandoned cart wheels. A gray wasteland of mud. There was poverty back in Biddeford, but it was a more decent poverty, with trees and bushes to soften the harshness.

"For a bit more money," Nora continued, "there are one-room apartments up on Clinton Street."

"Could I still work for you, after I move, and earn something toward the rent?"

Nora chuckled. "I'm sorry, love, but there's no extra money. I give Mamie the leftovers, ever since that lout of a husband deserted her, with nine mouths to feed."

Anne had seen a slight, dark-haired woman who changed the bed clothes and emptied the slop pails each morning but never spoke, never raised her eyes.

Nora thought a minute, index finger on her lips. "I might be able to do the same for you, that I might. A little meat and potatoes now and then. You see, everything is charged to Curran's. Butcher, grocer, laundry, coal, kerosene—everything. All the money is handled at the main office. I get a pittance of salary each month."

"Wouldn't you think, with Liam having been promoted to foreman, that he could afford a bit more than the regular workers?"

"Foreman? That spit of a boy, a foreman? Ha! Anne, Anne. Where did you ever get that notion?"

"In a letter he wrote me, a few months before we were married."

"Wrote you, did he? Wrote you a letter?" Nora laughed in disbelief. "Oh, my! As if any of the crowd that lives here can scratch more then his name. You've really been had there, my girl. Well, that explains a lot of it. All this time I've been trying to figure out how the likes of you got paired up with the likes of him."

Stunned, Anne turned away and fled the kitchen.

A knot of fear twisted in Anne's stomach as she knelt at the small attic window. She'd cleaned the glass with vinegar water and newspapers, polished it until it sparkled. Today, her mind was so blurred that she could not see the river or anything else. She continued to stare until she began to see flashes of sunlight that shimmered across the rippled water and danced on the river. The painful knot inside her began to unwind. She wanted the river to murmur to her as her mother had done. Her mother would press her close, stroke her back, and softly hum, "Yes…yes…yes." Anne felt the river drawing her out of the attic. The rough wood of the window sill no longer pricked her forearms, nor was the floor cold beneath her knees. The river enfolded her and she felt safer than she had since her mother died. Her mind drifted into an unfocused calm, without thought or care.

Gradually, she began to tell the river about the awful mistake she had made. That she had married a man who cared nothing for her, as she cared nothing for him. A man, who deceived her, lied to her. With whom she must live for the rest of her life. Bear his children.

For reasons beyond her understanding, she'd suggested they write to each other. Perhaps she was clinging to the memory of an evening of dancing and laughter, to a world beyond Chestnut Grove. Maybe she had believed that it would help her prepare for a suitable partner's appearance. His proposal of marriage had come as a shock to her. However, the opportunity to begin a new life down in Haverstraw had been enticing.

Tears began to stream down her cheeks. Her shoulders shook and once more the splintery wood stung her arms, the floor chilled her knees. When the tears stopped, Anne rose from the window, wiped her face on her sleeve, bent her head to avoid low-hanging rafters, and descended the narrow staircase.

She found Nora in the kitchen mixing flour and water in a crockery bowl to make gravy for the stew.

After the meal was over, Anne scraped a brush inside the large pot, dislodging particles of burned potato and meat that had stuck to its bottom.

"Tomorrow, remind me to show you where I keep the extra quilts. They should be aired before we put them on the beds."

When there was no answer, Nora looked over and saw Anne's crumpled face. She crossed over to the sink, took the brush from Anne's hand.

"Sit," she insisted. "Right now, you are going to sit down here and talk to me." She spoke firmly but quietly, aware that some men might have lingered in the dining room. She pushed Anne into one chair and pulled another one close so the two women were facing.

Anne began to weep. "I got myself into this, now I have to make the best of it." Her sobs choked off further words

Nora reached over and stroked Anne's arm. "You've stuck it out longer than I thought you would. After I saw that dress in your trunk...."

Anne could not speak, could not raise her head, shaking it back and forth.

The two women sat for a while. Anne finally brushed away her tears, looked up and forced a smile to Nora, who took her hand.

"Anne, love, there might be a small apartment down along the river in Grassy Point. I'll look into it tomorrow. His nibs will just have to have to come up with a bit more money."

Anne spoke in a low voice so it would not carry into the next room.

"There are hours in the day when you don't need me. All the time I've wasted at the library. Help me find a job."

"We better talk in my bedroom." She nodded toward the dining room. "And perhaps you'll tell me where you got that dress."

17

The following morning when Liam leapt from the bed and clattered down the narrow staircase, Anne feigned sleep. She lay in the still dark attic and considered what she discovered yesterday and what she would do about it.

She thought about the bank account up in Quebec and Uncle Henri's wedding gift of her aunt's jewelry, hidden at the bottom of her trunk. Now and then, when Nora was not around, Anne slipped the maroon leather box from where she had buried it under her clothes and admired the pearl necklaces and gold earrings, the diamond brooch and glittering rings she would never have an occasion to wear. Gazed at them and knew that Quebec had not been a dream. Anne mentioned neither the bank account nor the jewelry when she had confided in Nora last evening. That money would never be spent, the jewelry never sold. It was like the ground beneath her feet. It kept her from despair.

She had to decide when to confront Liam. He was always in a rush. If what Nora said was true, and Anne believed it was, then who had written the letters? Who had read her letters to Liam? The name "Schoolmaster" came to her. Of course. His best man, Ned. That's who it was. No wonder Ned could not look her in the eye. More questions began to form. Was it Liam who dictated the words to Ned or were they simply from Ned's imagination? And most important of all, which one, Liam or Ned, decided to write the letters A.M.D.G.? How naive she was, to have assumed he was invoking God as a blessing on his marriage proposal.

She was married to a fraud, as illiterate as her father and her brothers. Worse, he was also a liar. Her father schemed and conspired, but he was honest. He never claimed to be more than he was. The attraction Liam once held for her had vanished. His charming vulnerability ceased to amuse her.

How was she to endure a lifetime of marriage to this man, this coarse and ignorant boy whose only goal in life was the accumulation of wealth and the prestige it bought? She might accept, as God's will, submission to her husband, but that possibility did not appeal to Anne. She preferred Nora's passionate advice. "Be proud of yourself. Hold your head up."

"Because men have all the say in this world doesn't make it right." Nora told Anne, "I've never forgotten a woman who spoke at the Waldron Opera House a few years back. Her name was Susan B. Anthony. She said it should be against the constitution that only men can vote. Oh, she stirred things up around here. The whole village was hopping, most people were angry. Hard to believe but the women were the worst. Father Grogan told them to abide by St. Paul instead of Susan B. Anthony, which settled it for most of the Catholics. I'll never forget her. Now love, don't let yourself be dragged down by the likes of Liam O'Connor. Hold that pretty head up high."

Anne turned back the bedcovers and began to gather her undergarments and work clothes, deciding the knit stockings could wait until she'd bathed. She slipped her bare feet into her shoes.

When she straightened up, she cracked her forehead against a rafter. Rubbing away the pain, she hurried down to Nora's bathroom. As Nora suggested, she would visit the shops along Main Street and Broadway and inquire about a job. Once that was settled, she would find Ned Walsh and ask him some questions.

18

Anne found it difficult to ask for work, to introduce herself and receive brusque, often rude replies, but found a job at the local laundry, which she had enjoyed visiting. It always put her in mind of Aunt Josie's clean basement where Celeste taught her to iron damask napkins, to transform damp, wrinkled cloth into crisp, smooth fabric.

When she dropped off the dirty sheets this particular Monday, Anne spoke to the owner behind the counter, explained the hours she was available, and was hired to begin working the following morning.

With that settled, her next task was to locate Ned Walsh. There was a bakery down the street from the laundry, Mardot's. Anne stepped inside, saw all the tantalizingly decorated pastries in the glass display cases, and promised herself a cream-filled napoleon when she received her first salary. She asked a smiling older man behind the counter if he knew the address of Farrelly's grocery store.

"Liz's?" He beamed. After wiping his hands on his apron, he pointed a finger in the direction of Broad Street. "Two blocks down. You can't miss it. There's a sign out front."

It was a two-story, white house with a glass-enclosed sun porch that ran along the front and side. Through the small-paned, casement windows, Anne saw shelves filled with cans and boxes. A path along the side of the house led to a slanting cellar door, one half of which was propped open. Several large beer kegs stood on the grass near the cellar's entrance.

As her determination to confront Ned wavered, Anne hesitated before climbing the wooden steps to the porch. Suppose he was not the one who had written Liam's letters? Suppose he flatly denied it?

The door to the grocery was half-open. She pushed it further and found herself facing a short, plump woman. A few wisps of blond hair escaped from a red bandana covering her head.

"Good morning, missus. What can I get for you today?"

"Does Ned Walsh work here?" Anne asked, and her resolve weakened even further.

"Indeed he does. I just sent him around to Maroney the butcher to pick up some soup bones. Is there anything I might do for you?"

"No, thank you." Anne turned and left, her cheeks warm.

Anne hurried away down the brick sidewalk, chiding herself for her timidity. The woman was a perfect stranger who knew nothing about her, nor the purpose of her visit.

Half a block from the boarding house was a secondhand store that Anne always passed on her way to the laundry. Today, she paused at the entrance. From a large clock that she could see through the glass window of the shop, she knew Nora did not expect her for a few more minutes, and stepped inside. The air had the same dusty smell as the attic where she slept.

Clothing hung on a rack along one wall, men's jackets, and women's long skirts. There was a counter on the opposite side of the store, with two men behind it, their heads bent as if studying something, unaware or unconcerned by her presence. She crossed to the clothing and examined a white organdy shirtwaist. Tiny tucks ran from the shoulders to a tapered waistline. She had no need for a fancy shirtwaist. Anne wandered among a jumble of chairs and table. She ran her fingertips across the top of one table; the veneer surface was badly chipped, its edge pocked with cigar burns. A tablecloth would cover that, she thought. She assumed a stern manner and approached the men. One of them lifted his head.

"What is the price on that table?" she asked, pointing.

"One dollar plus fifty cents. If you take the four chairs with it, I'll give you the whole lot for three dollars."

"And...do you sell beds?"

"Not many. Beds are scarce in Haverstraw. You need a mattress, too?"

"Certainly."

"Look over in that corner, past the clothing. If you find something you like, tell me."

He turned back to whatever it was that engrossed him and his companion. They continued to speak quietly to each other while she examined the beds.

Anne thanked the men and left the store, excited at the prospect of furnishing her first home. Later, they'd bring everything with them to Chestnut Grove. As she stepped briskly along, Anne realized she was humming, and she laughed at herself.

19

Liam gloated, "By next week, Tim McNabb and I will own shares in Mrs. McCauley's schooner."

"How much are you taking out of your savings?"

"Not a bit. I told you. I'm selling the parcel of land up in Chestnut Grove."

"I see," Ned said, although he did not. "And did you get your price?"

"The bank has offered me fifteen hundred dollars, and will loan us another fifteen." Liam smirked.

Ned's sense of remorse, the awareness that he had participated in a farce and misled the lovely Anne, had lain quiet for a while, overcome by his powerlessness. Now the tormenting guilt drove him.

"Do you remember I offered to buy that land from you?"

"That's right, you did. But can you come up with fifteen hundred dollars, before next week?"

"You'll have it Friday." Ned spoke with more confidence than he felt.

That night, he and Liz sat at the kitchen table. She sliced apples while Ned shined his best shoes, the ones he'd bought with money his parents had given him for his ordination. Satisfied, Ned collected the brushes, paste, and polishing rags into a small wooden box and returned the box to the closet under the sink.

It was the interlude between supper and the opening of the saloon, when Ned usually read the newspaper. Tonight he put the paper aside and began to drum his fingertips on the table-top.

"What's worrying you?" Liz asked.

"I'm wondering if I could get a loan from you. It might take me two or three years, but I swear you'll get every penny back."

"You're one of the most honest men I've ever met. There's not a doubt in my mind about that. How much do you need?"

"One thousand dollars?"

"Mother of God!"

"I want to buy fifty acres of farmland upstate. I'll give you a note that says it is yours if the loan is not paid off in three years, or if I die in the meantime."

"What am I going to do with fifty acres of farmland? And up-state, to boot?"

"Rockland Savings and Loan would buy it from you today."

"I don't suppose you want to tell me what's going on here?"

"Liz," he pleaded.

"Oh, I forgot to mention. A young woman stopped in at the store yesterday and asked about Ned Walsh. I told her you were off to the butcher. She was very pretty. Spoke with an attractive little accent. Might she be Liam O'Connor's new bride?"

Ned lay on his cot, his left arm over his eyes, trying to rest before going downstairs but his mind would not permit rest. Anne came looking for him. Why? Was she in trouble? Had Liam told her about the farm, that he wanted to buy it? Ned's plan was to keep it until he had paid Liz back, then give it to Anne. He was glad he'd been out when she came by. The thought of facing her alarmed him. One day when she came into the library he'd hid-den in the bookstacks until he could slip out with only a premptory nod in her direction. But still, if she were in any sort of trouble, he wanted to help.

20

The moist air in the dimly lit back room of the laundry put Anne in mind of the textile mill. Three young women, wearing black rubber aprons, stood in the midst of a cluster of tubs. A large wringer was fastened to the rim of one tub, much larger than the one Aunt Josie's laundress, with Celeste's aid, had struggled with each washday. The tallest of the three women rotated the long crank handle, while the shortest one lifted a dripping sheet from the sudsy water and fed it between the rollers. A third woman received the damp sheet and guided it into an adjoining tub. Their lively conversation stopped when they noticed the approach of the owner and Anne.

"Kitty, Tess, Molly. This is Anne. She will be working with you. Kitty, you show her what to do." Before the owner left she handed Anne a black apron.

The three women measured Anne with hostile stares. Her inclination to greet them was rebuffed by Kitty's growl. "So get on with it. Give us a hand over here." She swept an arm toward the tubs.

Anne glanced around the room in search of the ironing area. Kitty growled again, "You best keep your wits about you, or that hair of yours might get caught in the wringer. Quick as a wink, it can pull the scalp right off your head." She looked at her two companions for confirmation and they nodded.

Anne made a quick braid of her hair and pinned it up, puzzled by her unfriendly reception. When she first saw and heard them giggling and chattering, she had anticipated joining them.

"Did you ever work in a laundry?" the third woman asked. Her tone was softer.

"Not in a real laundry like this one, but I've done ironing."

"Listen to her," Kitty jeered. " Do you hear the way she speaks? She's a foreigner. Where are you from?" she demanded.

"I grew up in Maine. We spoke French."

"She's a *frog*. A *mademoiselle*." Kitty's laugh was snide, unpleasant.

She assigned Anne to the most strenuous task: feeding the water-logged sheets into the wringer. This required leaning and twisting her body. Soon her shoulders and her back began to ache. And the top strap of the apron chaffed against her neck.

How foolish and ignorant she had been. To compare a public laundry with Aunt Josie's basement, where time had passed quickly as she ironed and Celeste entertained her with stories.

When the three women announced it was lunchtime, they stepped out a back door into the drying yard where damp sheets billowed from rope lines, and left Anne to tend the simmering starch. Kitty had mixed powdered starch and a cube of bluing into cold water in an oblong copper boiler that sat on top of a low, two-burner stove. She handed Anne a long wooden paddle. "Stir it until it thickens, then turn off the gas. And don't let me find any lumps in it."

Anne was tempted to walk away, there and then, but the thought of the mess she would cause if she abandoned the cooking starch held her. Her shoes were soaked and her feet hurt from standing in one spot for so long. Every part of her body was sore, and she was famished. She had not thought to bring a lunch.

The following morning, Anne knelt at the attic window to gaze out at the river. She felt nourished by it, protected. Fingers of white mist hung like a fringe over the slate surface. A man rowed from a hidden point on the shore out to where the water was deeper, and began to drop lines over the side. As she watched him, she reviewed her day at the laundry and heard again Kitty's caution about the wringer.

"...it can pull the scalp right off your head."

Her hair had become a bother, a chore finding both the time and the place to wash and dry it. What would have been unthinkable a year ago now became desirable. Long hair belonged on Anne-from-Quebec but was a girlish indulgence for a laundress in Haverstraw. She suspected Liam would be upset if she were to cut it off. That settled it.

It was unbecoming of her, but she would enjoy his displeasure. It is my hair, she told herself. He does not own it. Once it is cut off, he can do nothing about it.

"No lady cuts her hair, " Nora exclaimed. She refused, at first, but agreed when Anne threatened to cut it herself and make a dreadful chop of it.

Nora first wove the curls into a thick braid which she tied at both ends with a slender ribbon. When she was finished, she gave Anne the hair. "Some day you will treasure this."

Later, Anne was determined to ignore her co-workers. She did not speak to them and avoided their eyes when she took up her station at the wringer.

"Look at this, girls," Kitty crowed. "She's cut off her auburn curls."

Anne ignored Kitty and plunged her arms into the sudsy wash water.

"So, Frenchie, are you going to sell it?" Tess asked.

Anne decided not to answer. Molly, the kindest of the three, spoke up.

"There's a wig maker down in Nyack who buys hair. I don't know how much he pays."

Anne looked at Molly, shrugged, and said nothing. Nora had had tears in her eyes. Was hair really so special? She was already uneasy about Liam's reaction.

In an attempt to provoke Anne, Kitty rained a barrage of slurs on everything French. On *frogs*. But she said nothing Anne had not heard before, back in Biddeford where the immigrant Irish had been determined to keep the newer immigrant French in their place. Anne found a way to ignore Kitty's abuse. As she handled the wet sheets, she went through each room in Aunt Josie's house, pictured each furnishing, the design of every carpet, the pattern and color of the drapes and the upholstery.

Finally bored with tormenting Anne, Kitty engaged the others in gossip about men and plans for the weekend. Tess had a new gentleman friend, and entertained Kitty with sarcastic comments about him.

"He says he has two tickets to the new show at the Waldron Opera House. Paid a dollar for them. I want to see his face when I tell him how, when I was a little girl, my father took me to the Broadway to see George M. Cohan. Imagine, the Waldron Opera House?"

Anne could not help listening to their conversation. She wondered why Tess accepted the attentions of a man whom she scorned.

"You can do better than him," Kitty said. "You're a good looking girl, when you put your mind to it."

Molly made several attempts to join the conversation. She was worried about her backyard. "It looks like an accordion out there, my ma says. She wants us to move but my father says where would we go. He says we don't need to worry. The brickyards know what they're doing."

"The brickyards don't give a fig for anything but clay," Kitty said. "Tell us, Frenchie, didn't you say you live on Allison Street, near the clay bank?"

Tess changed the subject when Anne remained silent. "Molly,

you always have sad stories. Give us a laugh. Tell us about your gentlemen friends."

Molly blushed and looked away.

After the three returned from their lunch, Anne walked to the front of the store and told the owner she was leaving. Despite probing as to her reason, Anne said no more than that.

"They're a tough bunch," the woman said, as she paid Anne her three dollars.

The napoleon she had promised herself now seemed a foolish waste of money.

"I quit, Nora. It was not at all what I expected. The girls were so unpleasant and I was miserable."

"Good for you," Nora agreed, as she rubbed ointment into Anne's reddened hands. "Why would you take any guff from a bunch of young harpies?" She clucked as she smoothed a hand over Anne's bobbed head. "It was such lovely hair." Nora pressed her index finger against her mouth and was silent for a while. Anne knew the wheels in Nora's head were turning.

"How about a job as a domestic? You've seen those big houses in the Heights, up along Hudson Avenue. Sometimes they hire couples as live-ins. The man drives their carriage, takes care of the horses and acts as a handyman. Liam's always looking for work, now that the yards are shut down for the winter. It should be easier driving a carriage than tramping six miles to Rockland Lake and back. With his room and board included, it should pay better than cutting ice. As you say, it would only be until spring." She pulled a handkerchief from her sleeve and wiped her eyes. "I don't want to see you leave. You're good company." She blew her nose.

"I have another problem. It embarrasses me to talk about it.... Strange stains on my underpants. For several weeks." An anxious look flashed across Nora's face. The older woman shoved her hand into the pocket of her long skirt, then thrust a fistful of dollar bills in Anne's hand. "Don't you waste another moment. You march yourself right up Main Street to Doctor Dillon and find out what's the matter."

The doctor's waiting room was crowded. Several times, Anne was tempted to leave. But Nora would ask what the doctor had to say. Her insistence that Anne speak to the doctor immediately worried Anne.

Doctor Dillon listened, his shoulder pressed against the wall of the room, arms crossed, his lips twisted in exasperation. He shook his head several times.

"You French gals, you take such risks for a few dollars. What can you expect?" he scolded.

Initially confused by his reaction, Anne grasped the implication of his remark. Mortified, she stuttered a protest.

"I am a married woman, doctor."

His eyebrows lifted, he grimaced.

"I see. So your husband has been careless? Well, don't bother to disrobe, I can't help you."

Anne fled the doctor's office, tears of shame and rage and disappointment blinding her. She stumbled down the the doctor's front steps and almost tripped, but caught herself by the hand-rail.

Anne hurried through the kitchen, passed Nora without speaking, climbed to the attic, and huddled against the window.

It was twilight. On the opposite shore lights glittered. Through the dusk she could see the outline of small fishing boats. Their bobbing lanterns winking like fireflies across the water. The steamboat, *Mary Powell*, turned from the main channel toward the Emeline Dock, her windows a brilliant yellow radiance in the gray night. Anne heard the ship's horn blare its arrival

Little more than a year had passed since Anne, dressed in a silk gown, had boarded the *Mary Powell* on her way to a church dance. In search of a new life, a better life. She had been foolish. To have thrown away her future on an impulse, on a whim.

Whether Liam could read or was a foreman meant little compared to this betrayal. It was too harsh, too cruel, to discover she must not conceive a child. Each time Liam had climbed on top of her and she turned her face away from his sour breath, Anne reminded herself that this was the price she must pay to bear a child. The child who would give meaning to her life. A daughter, perhaps, whom she would name Emilie, after Paul's daughter.

Darkness fell and though she could no longer see, the river pursued its restless journey over and about, through and past whatever it encountered, toward the sea.

The river drew her into its depths where, drifting and floating, she forgot the pre-dawn whistles, the strangers' fingers that groped through her petticoats and pinched her body, the loneliness, the longing, and the barren years that loomed ahead.

Tomorrow, were she to walk out to the end of the Emiline Dock and sit, with her legs dangled over the side, and then slip down into the welcoming water, she knew the river would embrace her and gently rock her into a dreamless sleep.

When Anne woke, the attic was dark. She rubbed the side of her face that had been pressed against the wooden frame of the window. Her knees and hips felt stiff when she rose from the frigid floor. She stooped as she felt her way past the mattresses to the stairwell.

"When you hurried past me without a word, I knew it meant trouble. Sit down now, and have your supper." The older woman took a plate of food from the oven and set it on the table. "Be careful, the plate is hot. Then, come into my bedroom and tell me everything."

After she related the doctor's report, Anne wondered aloud whether she would bother to confront Liam about his lies. What would it accomplish, to list his failings? The reality was that she was his wife and that would never change. She had best accept the fact, be reconciled to the price she must pay for the reckless choice she had made, and accept whatever the future held. With one exception... she would not harm a child.

"How will I ever convince Liam? He'd have to admit this is his fault. You know him as well as I. He's so thick-headed, he'll never listen."

"Well I can think of one person he'll have to listen to. You go have a talk with Father Grogan. Surely he'll say it's a sin to cause a child to be born deformed."

Father Grogan was the pastor at St. Peter's. A weight lifted from Anne's heart. For all his bluster, Liam would never face down a priest.

"Nora, you are a treasure. I can't bear the thought of talking about this to another man, even if he is a priest. But if Liam will have to accept whatever the church says is right, I will have to do my part."

The priest's housekeeper left Anne in a small room, with two straight chairs, a table, and a lamp that gave off a soft pink light. A sheer curtain hung at the single window. The hall she had first entered, and the room, immaculately clean, reminded Anne of the convent in Quebec. The housekeeper said Father Grogan would be down shortly, and left, closing the door. Anne studied the lamp's bulbous glass shade, decorated with overblown white roses on a cerise background. It most likely was a donation, for it was not in keeping with the simple wooden furniture and bare floor. The door opened and Father Grogan entered the room. Although Anne had not met the pastor before, she recognized him from Mass.

"Please be seated," he said, as he took the other chair. "How can I help you?"

Anne did not take her eyes off her hands, which she clasped

tightly in her lap, while she explained, as delicately as she could, the purpose of her visit. When she finished, the priest made no comment. She glanced up. He seemed deep in thought, weighing his response.

"The marriage vow is sacred," he began. "Your body now belongs to your husband, as his belongs to you."

Anne was astonished. *Love, honor, and obey—sickness or health—until death.* That is what she had promised. Not ownership of her body. The idea was repugnant.

"And therefore," he continued, "you cannot refuse your husband when he claims his rights." He paused, then continued. "Mrs. O'Connor, some things you must leave in God's hands. And pray for the courage to accept His will."

Anne was stunned at the enormity of what was being asked of her. "I would think the health of a child would be more important than a husband's rights."

The priest grimaced and squinted, as if struggling with his thoughts.

"There is another option. Your husband could forfeit his rights. It might be difficult, but others have done so." He shrugged.

Anne had heard enough. The church had nothing to offer. Nothing she could use to convince Liam.

"Father, I thank you for your time."

She rose to leave. The priest stood also with his hand extended. She shook it.

"I will keep you in my prayers," he said. "But, before you go, may I ask about your accent? Are you from France, or from Canada?"

"I studied in Quebec, Father." Impulsively she added, "I attended the Ursuline Convent and, after graduation taught school up in Beaupré."

The priest did not try to conceal his surprise. "Indeed. So, you are a teacher."

At first, Anne thought he had not understood her, for his head was cocked and he stared at her. Again, he seemed to be weighing his words before he spoke.

"Forgive me, Mrs. O'Connor. I was recalling a conversation I had with the principal of our school only yesterday. The sister who teaches first grade there will have to leave after Christmas to care for her elderly mother. I'm wondering if you might be interested in the position."

21

That night when Liam turned to Anne to initiate the wordless ritual of increasingly urgent grunts and jerking movements that left a trail of moisture across her thigh when he collapsed off her, she was prepared. She sat on the side of the mattress, fully clothed.

"Not tonight. I'm not well."

He misunderstood that it was her time of the month, and punched his fist into the mattress. She was tempted to let him think she had her flow, but that meant several more days of fretting, postponing what must be said..

She pulled the quilt around her shoulders, for the attic was bitter cold, and sent a prayer to St. Anne for courage.

She struggled to keep her voice firm, but despite her efforts began to sob. "I'm no longer clean. You have made me unclean." She did not know how else to say it.

"What? What have I done?" He turned in the bed. "Are you accusing me of something?" There was anger as well as confusion in the question.

Encouraged that he was listening, had actually heard what she said, Anne continued.

"My sickness came from you. From our being together. " She hurriedly recounted her visit to Dr. Dillon, avoiding the insult about French women.

In the dim light of the lantern, she saw Liam's mouth sag open. He sat back on the mattress. Unsure of what to say next, Anne sat on the bed and waited. After a period of silence, Liam groaned. He reached across and fumbled for her hand. He had never taken her hand before.

"I'm sorry. I'm truly sorry."

His contrition disarmed her. It was so unexpected that her determination wavered. Anne saw again the boy who'd arrived at her father's cabin shivering from the cold. There was no bravado in his voice tonight.

"My mates. They insisted I have a woman, while I was still single. My last fling, they said. My first fling, it was. They took me up the river to Diamond Street."

"My arms will never hold my child." She began to sob again.

"It might be a mistake."

"The doctor was certain."

Despite her misery, Anne realized that, at last, she and Liam were speaking to each other openly. She did not want to spoil the moment with her other complaints about letters and promotions. She considered telling him about her visit to Father Grogan and what he said about a wife's obligation to her husband. And how a man might choose to forfeit his rights. But something made her hesitate. Something told her to wait.

She patted his hand. "We'll talk more about this, but not right now. You need to get some sleep."

Anne lay awake, for hours it seemed. Her mind jumping from one idea to another. It kept returning to the way she and Liam had talked to each other. This was a different person, one she could reason with. She felt a renewed sense of commitment to their marriage, a determination to overlook the past and begin anew. They would help each other, look out for each other, forgive each other.

She made a promise to herself and to her marriage that she would stop thinking about Paul. A week or so after Liam had begun to sleep with her, Anne began to pretend that it was Paul who lay in the bed beside her. She'd pretended it was Paul she had married, Paul who would be coming home to her at the end of the day. Paul would visit the library with her, suggest books to read. One Sunday Liam had asked where she had put his heavy sweater and she replied, "Over there, Paul, in that gray box by the window." He'd stared at her. 'You called me Paul.' She shrugged and turned away. Liam was not amused. "Who the hell is Paul?" he demanded.

"A cousin. Back in Biddeford. We grew up together."

When Liam entered Farrelly's saloon the following Monday for his usual pint, he was met with guffaws and snickers. Prior to his arrival, Tim Maloney overheard Jack Reilly telling Tom Nolan that a new customer was seen on the second floor of the American Hotel Sunday evening. In a matter of minutes, the whole room rocked with the news. That address was notorious for perfumed guests who arrived with the Friday night boat from New York City. All weekend long, men with a week's pay in their pockets lined its halls, impatiently waiting their turn. When Liam realized he was the target of the good-natured ribbing, he smirked and shrugged, which made the men roar louder. His hands on his hips, he strutted about like a rooster, with his chest out, chin up and eyes shut tight.

Tom Nolan leaned across the bar and asked Ned, who was keeping busy polishing spots off glasses, "I've seen his wife. With a fine-looking woman like that at home, what's he doing at the American Hotel?"

"I've no idea." Ned kept his head down to hide his indignation. This did not bode well for Anne or their marriage. Ned debated whether or not he would demand an explanation from Liam. He was turning the matter over in his mind when Liam appeared at the bar.

"Will you have the money?" Liam fiddled with his pipe. He knocked it empty, then tamped tobacco into the bowl, all the while avoiding Ned's eyes.

"I have it, upstairs, under my mattress. I made an appointment for us to meet at McCann's office tomorrow at three o'clock."

"No need for lawyers. You just scratch out my name and write in yours."

"For so much money, I need legal advice. I already discussed it with Mr. McCann."

The following afternoon Liam and Ned presented themselves at the offices of Patrick J. McCann.

The lawyer studied the document Liam handed him. "This is written in French," he said. "I'll have to have my assistant translate it." He disappeared, closing the door to his office behind him.

Liam reached inside his shirt, pulled out the small leather sack and dangled it at Ned. "Remember this? My veil. A guarantee of my good fortune. By Friday night, McNabb and I will be part owners of a schooner and drinks will be on the house." Preoccupied with his bragging, he missed the look of contempt in Ned's eyes.

"I don't want to drink with you. Our friendship is finished." The hostility in Ned's voice erased Liam's grin but, before he could respond, the lawyer strode back into the room. With a shake of his head, McCann tossed the paper onto his cluttered desk.

"What you have here is an agreement to lease, not to sell, the property," he said. "You'll need the owner's permission before this can be transferred."

Ned's mind traveled back to the wedding reception when Anne's father, waving an envelope, had called for quiet and made his announcement. The burst of approval from the French-speaking guests led Ned to assume that the father had given his daughter and her new husband an extravagant gift. '*Cinquante arpents—cinquante arpents,*' the crowd repeated to each other. 'Fifty acres'? Had the older man exaggerated his generosity? Would the cheering have been as loud had they known it was not an outright gift of the land?

The afternoon when Liam had brought him the paper, Ned skimmed through it. "It says here, '*cinquante arpents*' and '*cinquante*' means fifty. '*Arpents*' must be the word for 'acres'." He could read classical French fairly well but his facility with the day to day language was rudimentary. He had no familiarity with legal terms, English or French. "Show this to Anne. She can tell you what it says." Obviously, Liam had not done this.

It took a few minutes for Liam to comprehend the impact of the lawyer's statement. "The bank agreed to buy it outright," he protested.

"Did the bank see this?" The lawyer waved the crumpled paper.

"I was to bring it with me on Friday."

"There is no way they can accept it without the written permission of Lucien Lessard. If you'd like, Mr. O'Connor, I would be glad to contact him for you."

Liam grabbed the piece of paper and stormed out of the office.

Ned followed at a distance, relieved that Liz would get her money back within the hour. It was wrong of him to take advantage of a kind-hearted widow with three children to raise. And it had been against his better judgment to assume so great a debt and deplete all his savings. But he would do so again, would do anything to help Anne.

Ned was torn between a certain satisfaction that Liam's plans had gone awry, and his concern for Anne. What would Liam do now? Move to Chestnut Grove? Gamble that the sun would shine and the rain fall in proper amounts at the proper times? Ned doubted this. Liam's sights were clearly on the bustling city with its promise of wealth.

Ned returned the money to Liz after supper and she accepted

it without comment. Not that she didn't lift an eyebrow.

"I owe you some sort of explanation." He took a deep breath. "It is all such a muddle. Let me begin with the young woman who came looking for me the other day."

He told her about Liam and the letters. How one look at Anne confirmed his worries but a cowardly fear of embarrassment kept him from speaking out in the church. And how her friend, Louise, after several glasses of wine, broke her promise to Anne by revealing her friend's past. He did not tell Liz about the wild attraction he fought in vain each time he saw Anne.

"You intended to buy the wedding gift and give it back to her?"

"I was frantic. I have to try to make up to her for what I've done and I don't know how."

"What's done is done. Leave them alone to work it out for themselves. Get on with your own life. I've noticed several of the women customers giving you the eye."

Ned tried to follow Liz's advice to stay out of it. Concentrate on his own affairs. But he had no other affairs to concentrate on. He had detached himself from everything. He had too much time for thinking. Hours alone in the grocery, shelving, sweeping, with only an occasional customer to break the silence. And long nights when sleep would not come.

Once he had prayed for guidance, but he no longer believed in prayer. He no longer believed in anything beyond what his hands could feel, his eyes could see.

22

Through his bedroom door, Ned heard metal grating against metal. Liz was building a fire in the stove before she left for early Mass. The children in their Sunday best would attend a later Mass under the supervision of the nuns. Ned threw back the covers. In spite of himself, he would to go to church.

By the time he was washed, dressed, and had made up his bed, Liz was long gone. The snow that had fallen during the night covered the dusty town with a spotless garment. In the sky across the Hudson, the sun cast gold and coral threads through a thin cover of clouds. The air was brisk. A mild breeze brushed his cheeks.

Ned climbed the stairs at the rear of the church to the empty choir loft, from which he could watch without being observed himself. Where he felt invisible, spectator rather than participant. Fortunately, in his rush he had grabbed his heavy jacket, for the choir loft was unheated.

So this was the new St. Peter's. The pride of Haverstraw. Built with donated bricks from every yard, regardless of the owners' religious persuasion, replacing an earlier, smaller church. There had been great fanfare in the village at its dedication several years ago.

The sanctuary, the raised area behind the communion rail,

was ablaze with candles. Gold leaf on four large candelabra and on the tabernacle picked up the flickering light An enormous crucifix hung over an ornate marble altarpiece that covered the back of the sanctuary. Gaslight shone from globes of cut glass along the walls of the church. Many of the women had black shawls draped around their head and shoulders. Among them he recognized Liz's feathered hat.

A hand bell was rung which drew Ned's attention back to the sanctuary. Two young boys emerged from the sacristy, each dressed in a starched white surplice over a long black cassock. They were followed by the celebrant in an embroidered mauve chasuble. Ah, Ned thought, purple—Advent.

"*Intribo ad altare Dei,*"" the priest chanted. *I will go in unto the altar of God.*

"*Ad Deum qui laetificat juventuitem meam*" Ned responded. *Unto God who giveth joy to my youth.*

A distant warm memory distracted him.

It was a Saturday morning when he was ten. His mother was ironing his cotton surplice. She stood in front of a padded board that was balanced between the top of two chairs, next to the stove where the irons were heated, a folded rag protected her palm from the hot handle. The iron thumped each time she set it down on the board. When it cooled, she returned that iron to the fire and picked up the second iron. She would wet her finger and quickly touch it to the sole of the second iron to test it.

Ned sat with his father at the kitchen table. They were rehearsing the Latin responses he had memorized phonetically, with no understanding of their meaning. Only that they were special and sacred. His father recited the priest's part and waited for Ned to answer. His mother, going about her tasks during the weeks of tutoring, had also learned the Latin. She hummed her approval each time Ned gave the proper response,

Finally, his father presented him to the parish priest, and he had become an altar boy. The following Sunday, in front of the entire parish, he first knelt in the sanctuary. His parents sat in the front pew and any time Ned hesitated, his mother softly called out his cue. Ned's father took her to task for this later. At the end of Mass, his mother and father put their arms around him and then hugged each other, proud of their son, reassured that they were good parents.

Even prouder when, at fifteen, he entered the seminary.

Ned noticed boot heels poking from the hem of the black cassocks. Underneath their outfits, they were, as he had been, just ordinary boys.

"*Christe, eleison.*" The boys' voices chorused the prayer without hesitation. Perhaps one of them suspected he had received the call. Be careful, Ned wanted to warn. Don't breathe a word to your mother. The joy in her eyes will settle it, will quash any doubt that might linger. Unless you are tripped up, dismissed, turned out with neither rhyme nor reason. The dust of the seminary shaken from your sandals. A wound Ned thought had healed with willed indifference, started to throb. He was grateful he was alone in the darkened choir loft. Unchecked tears ran down his cheeks.

Why? he asked. Why? He had convinced himself he no longer cared about the why. It was the how that enraged him. But now the need to know why burned in him as fiercely as the afternoon the head of the order told him he would not be ordained.

Ned wiped his face, rose and turned to leave the choir loft but stopped when he saw Anne. She sat in a rear pew that had been concealed from him by the front of the loft. In her gray fur cape and matching hat, the elegant tilt of her head reminded him of the first time he had seen her, poised and exquisitely gowned. Ned's heart began to thump in his chest.

He returned to his pew but knelt this time, so he could look over the balcony and watch her. His conscience began to scold him. She was a married woman and he had no business staring at her. Mortified, he sat back in the pew.

Please, he asked, quiet my heart. Take away this terrible attraction I feel for another man's wife. It was the first real prayer he had uttered in many years. The joy he had known chanting psalms, singing hymns of submission and adoration, had been lost. All those days, those years, all those words, repeated again and again until they had become a part of him, had vanished.

The congregation stood for the reading of the Gospel, and Ned stood as well. For a brief moment, he allowed his eyes to flicker down and over to where Anne stood. Her hair was different. Ringlets curled around the edges of the fur hat. Missing was the abundance of glossy, auburn curls she twisted up into a charming fluff. Her lovely hair had been cut. A further step in the grinding down process he saw ahead of her. Would she try to bury herself, as he had, to avoid further disappointment and hurt? Concern for this young woman overpowered his self-pity and fear of pain.

Freed from formal, orchestrated words, he whispered, to whomever might hear him.

"Please allow me to help her. Show me what I can do."

Ned felt a peaceful, relaxing calm settle on him.

"*Lavabo inter innocentes manus meas—I will wash my hands among the innocent....*" The priest was about to consecrate the bread and wine.

He watched as individuals left their pews and approached the communion rail, where the priest, moving from left to right, placed a host on each tongue. A yearning to receive the Eucharist stirred in Ned. But he was not in the state of grace. He must first present himself to a priest for absolution.

Ned remained in the choir loft until the church was empty, to avoid both Anne and Liz. When he finally slipped out, the two of them were there on the sidewalk, talking. Ned tried to reenter the church, but Liz had seen him.

"Ned. Come join us."

23

Startled by Liz's call, Anne looked over her shoulder. Ned walked toward them, his mouth clamped shut, his shoulders hunched, his body drawn back inside his coat. His face revealed neither pleasure nor anticipation. His gruff manner the morning he took the meal pails from her and his snub of her in the library, together with his aloofness at the wedding, and his reluctance to speak to her today, led Anne to believe he did not approve of her, or else he found her tiresome. Yet, the day up on High Tor, he had been pleasant.

Liz either failed to observe or chose to ignore his discomfort. "This is the young lady who asked for you at the store last week. We've just introduced ourselves."

Ned raised the soft cap he was wearing, and bowed slightly. "Mrs. O'Connor."

Liz gave him a push on his arm. "I'm surprised to see you here. Surprised and delighted."

Anne seized the opportunity. He might not approve of her, but he owed her an apology.

"They call you the Schoolmaster. Is that not so, Ned?"

Ned mumbled a reply into his collar.

"Indeed they do, missus," Liz said. "And with good reason. Whenever he has a free moment, Ned's nose is in a book." From the tone of her voice, it was obvious that Liz was fond of Ned.

"It appears to me that some of the men are illiterate," Anne persisted. "Perhaps they ask you for write letters for them?"

"All the time, missus," Liz answered. "All the time. They line up outside my kitchen door for him to finish eating his supper."

Ned looked directly at Anne and his eyes made her want to turn away. Their expression, ragged and searching, scared her. They held neither anger nor hostility. Only a terrible pain.

"God forgive me, for what I did," he pleaded. "I had no idea the great harm I would cause."

Anne shook her head for him to stop. His admission and contrition was enough. Protestations of good intentions would be meaningless. The damage was done.

"Come back to the house with us, missus," Liz suggested, "and perhaps we can sort this all out. I baked three apple pies yesterday. The young ones will have eaten one by now but that leaves enough for us."

The morning had taken on an unreal quality. Here she was walking down Broadway with Ned and this pleasant woman, as though they were good friends. The clouds had blown away and a blazing sun had begun its climb through an azure sky. A thin coverlet of snow blanketed the village. Bare tree limbs and privet hedges were laced in white.

When they reached the corner of Jefferson and Rockland, Ned pointed out a large fissure that separated the brick sidewalk from the roadbed. Had it not been for his careful observation, they would never have noticed it under the snow.

"The yards have dug too close," he commented. "By spring, when the ground softens, this area might go down."

"But there are homes here, and stores, and..." Anne's confusion was met with a cynical laugh from Ned.

"The brickyards will say their hands are clean. Each owner has been offered a price, only for the land, not the house on it. Far less than what they'd have to pay to buy elsewhere. I've heard Curran has plans to move your boarding house to a vacant lot over on Division Street."

"Nora said the same thing. I've noticed cracks in the backyard of the boarding house." Anne was dismayed.

"There's plenty of clay to harvest from the river. DeNoyelles proved it. They built a coffer dam along the shoreline years ago. Found finer clay than what's up here. But it's easier to keep on digging out the clay bank. The owners are so powerful, no one can touch them."

"Didn't a man recently win a court case against a brickyard?"

"He won in court but the yard is still digging clay at the very same spot. That's nothing new."

Liz broke in. "Look around you. Everywhere you look, you see what bricks mean to Haverstraw. Look at the stables, the shipyards, the machine shops, and the dry goods stores. And the village is still growing. All because of bricks. Nyack can't compare to us. We have three hotels. People know that without the brickyards we'd be just a sleepy river town like all the others. Come on, now. Enough gloomy talk."

Ned took her hat and cape, brushing flour from the kitchen chair before he offered it to her. He'd become a different person. It was as if his admission of blame had released whatever restrained him earlier. Perhaps what she perceived as aloofness may have been only reticence.

"Mrs. O'Connor, I'd like you to meet Robbie." Ned lifted a small boy onto his shoulders. The youngster clapped his hands against Ned's cheeks. Ned growled and the delighted child repeated the gesture. "He's a great one for smashing my face, though his mother does not approve of it," Ned said and swung the boy back to the floor, his affection for the youngster obvious.

Kate and Theresa dropped curtsies when their mother presented them to Anne, then turned to their task of setting the table.

"When you finish there, help Robbie on with his felt boots," Liz called to Kate, "and don't forget mittens. Theresa, I want no sliding in the snow in your best coat. Come home first and change."

In a flurry of squeals and assurances, the three set out for the children's Mass. Liz, her curly blond hair awry, set a fresh pot of tea on the table and sank into a chair beside Anne. "Now let us talk."

Ned began by describing Liam's sheepish request for help. "It seemed harmless at first. Good fun."

"As it was for me," Anne said. "Something to look forward to."

"When he asked me to write about the promotion to foreman, it was the boast of a man who wanted to impress a young lady. Still only a game. Not until he asked me write the proposal of marriage did it bother me. I insisted he let me write the truth, but he put me off."

"Liam is clever that way." Anne glanced over at Liz who was listening intently. "Ned, the blame is mine as much as yours. My first instinct was to refuse Liam. He had none of the qualities I expected to find in a husband. But then I considered my life and my prospects and it seemed a fair bargain. I believe I was more anxious to live in Haverstraw than I was to become Liam's wife."

There was silence for several minutes. Anne sifted through what she had heard herself admit.

Liz picked up their cups and tossed the dregs into the sink. She poured each a fresh cup of tea and placed the pot on the table.

Ned cleared his throat and began to speak in a quiet, halting manner that captured Anne's full attention.

"At the wedding your friend, Louise, insisted I dance with her despite my protests that I have two left feet. She'd had quite a bit of the wine. I was trying to make conversation, and asked a question or two and your secret spilled out of her. When your friend realized she'd broken her promise to you, she pleaded with me, asked me to swear I'd never repeat it. I don't know which of us was the more horrified. I'd done even worse harm than I'd thought."

"I've wanted to talk about it, about Quebec, but how could I? It feels good to be myself again. I'm not even angry with you anymore."

Liz and Ned looked at each other, then at her. They nodded and smiled.

"The pastor of St. Peter's has offered me a position teaching at the parish school," Anne announced. "And I've just decided to accept."

She could not decipher the expression on Ned's face. Was it encouragement or was it concern?

"I don't care what Liam thinks," she continued.

"Those fifty acres up in Chestnut Grove?" Ned asked.

Anne listened with disbelief as Ned revealed the events that had led up to the scene in the lawyer's office.

"He was going to sell the land to you? And buy shares in a schooner?"

"If ever Liam had a comeuppance, it was when the lawyer discovered the land was leased, not sold, to him. Liam was bragging that his future had unfolded at last. The schooner was going to lift him off the clay bank and sail him down the river to his golden city of dreams."

Anne cocked her head as she absorbed these facts. "He had no intention of moving to Chestnut Grove this spring. And you're telling me that what my father gave us was only the lease to the land? Liam never showed me the paper. I did wonder where my father found the money to buy it. "

She felt a mixture of relief and annoyance. However, the possibility of not returning to Chestnut Grove delighted her.

Liz rapped a spoon on the table. "What are Liam's plans now, Ned?"

"I'd told him, even before the lawyer surprised us with the news, that our friendship was finished. We've not spoken since."

Anne was really thinking out loud, when she asked, "How will he take it then, his wife a teacher? On top of all this?"

"If you'll permit me, I'll speak to him first. There are other matters I need to discuss with him."

"I would be grateful."

His eyes were no longer raw or pleading. They had a familiar softness. In the space of a few hours, her estimation of Ned Walsh had reversed itself completely. She knew she was as safe with Liz and Ned as she was with Nora.

"Nora! Gracious," she exclaimed, as she pushed back her chair. "I must hurry. Nora is expecting my help with Sunday dinner."

Liz and Ned helped her on with her cape and Liz shook her hand.

"You're most welcome to visit with us anytime, Mrs. O'Connor." Liz hesitated, then added, "Would you and your husband join us for Christmas dinner?"

When thumps outside the kitchen door and childish voices interrupted her, she added, "If you can stand the racket around here. "

At that the back door opened and her three youngsters, coats and mittens covered with snow, burst into the kitchen. "Boots outside. Wet boots outside," Liz shouted.

"That would be lovely, Mrs. Farrelly," Anne said. "We have no plans for Christmas."

24

Anne had just carried a large platter of roasted lamb into the dining room. As she leaned between two of the men to lay it at the center of the table, a hand grasped her thigh. Instinctively, she let out a cry and the platter fell from her hands. Some of the men guffawed. She looked over at Liam and was astonished to see confusion on his face. She was further astonished to hear him snarl, "Keep your hands off my wife." He glowered at the guilty party who offered back a sheepish grin. All conversation had ceased. The room was still silent when Anne returned with a steaming bowl of mashed turnips. The offender took it from her mumbling, "Thank you, missus."

The first time Liam had stood up for her in front of his mates. It was certainly a day of surprises.

She had to decide when it would be best to speak to Liam. She wanted to talk about finding a better place to live, and tell him she might teach at St. Peter's School. They were husband and wife. If she knew his secrets, he was entitled to know hers. Most of them, anyway.

In the peace and quiet of the kitchen, Anne and Nora ate their dinner together.

"Your gravy is like velvet. Mine always has a hundred lumps."

"Remind me. When I make it again, I'll show you my tricks."

"Since next Sunday is Christmas Eve, will you cook your usual big dinner then and another one, the following day, on Christmas?"

"Never. Christmas is always my day off. I spend it with my niece, Sally, down in Nyack. I'll have Mamie Finnigan in to serve them leftovers. What about you? Are you going to your father's?"

"Liam and I will go up on New Year's Day. It's a French tradition to visit your father on the first day of the New Year to receive his blessing. Perhaps my father's neighbor, Mr. Lessard, will have him over for Christmas."

She had mailed her father a Christmas card a week ago. She also sent one to Uncle Henri in Toronto, as well as one to Louise. "And," she drawled, "Liam and I are invited out for Christmas dinner."

Anne put down her fork, wiped her mouth with a napkin and hunched closer to the older woman. "You'll never believe what happened this morning."

"I wondered where you were off to. You usually come straight back from church."

While Nora finished eating, Anne described how, after Mass, she was leaving the church when Liz Farrelly introduced herself. When Anne reached the part about Liam's futile attempt to sell the land up in Chestnut Grove, she waited for Nora's reaction.

"He's a corker, that one." Nora pushed herself back from the table. "Well, if he can't sell it, I guess he'll have to farm it." She gathered their knives and forks and the soiled dishes and carried them over to a pan of sudsy water. "You do have bad luck, though. Here you are, offered a proper job, a chance to teach, instead of washing dirty laundry or cooking and cleaning, and you have to pass it up to go live on a farm and slop hogs. "

"I won't do it. I'm not leaving here." The words popped out of Anne's mouth. Until the moment she heard herself say the words out loud, Anne had not known she could refuse. Again, she felt energy stir in her. Of course she would not leave Haverstraw. Liam was even less interested in moving to Chestnut Grove than she was. So, that decision was made, the matter settled. She wanted to slip upstairs and tell the river she was staying. Listen for its comforting "yes...yes...yes...."

"I don't know how I'll tell my father. What to say when he askes about our plans. He'll want to start plowing as soon as the soil is ready. Should I tell him straight away and risk his blessing, or wait?" She was not asking Nora, only chasing her own thoughts. "How foolish I am. As soon as we walk through the door, his first question will be about our returning. Since Liam doesn't understand French, it will be left for me to explain. Of course, I'm not certain that Liam will even agree to accompany me.

"New Year's Day is pretty quiet around here. The men stay in bed and nurse their sore heads. All business shuts down for the holiday and there won't be any work so you just may have a traveling companion."

"My father won't like it when we return the gift, which we must. He'll be angry. But I won't let that change my mind." She felt the energy pulsing through her. She was not afraid of her father. Hadn't been, since the Easter morning she'd run from him to hide in the glen.

"Nonetheless, despite everything, I cannot forget that he is my father. He deserves, if no longer my obedience, at least my respect. I will ask for his blessing. And he may not give it."

25

Ned whistled as he hustled about the grocery, sweeping the linoleum floor, stocking the shelves, totaling new accounts. He felt as if he had been rescued from a dungeon. He no longer looked away when customers spoke to him, not even when one woman, with a coquettish smile, asked him to recommend a brand of tea. He didn't stammer when younger women searched his face while he counted out their change. He greeted them by name as they entered the grocery. He asked how their day was going, inquiring the name of the child at their knee. It unsettled some of them; often it was they who stammered as they rearranged their opinion of him. Throughout the day, Ned debated how best to approach Liam, what words to use.

That night, as soon as the younger man entered the saloon, Ned called him over. Liam's face was a mask. The cocky grin was missing. He avoided Ned's eyes.

"I understood you wanted nothing more to do with me." His voice was petulant, injured.

"I did say that. I was very angry," Ned conceded. "Furious at the disrespect you show your wife."

"You've always had your eye on her, haven't you?" Liam spoke with the old defiance, as he struggled to gain the upper hand.

"I have something important to discuss with you. Can you come by Liz's after work tomorrow? We'll talk in my room where there's privacy."

"Maybe," Liam replied. With a sullen shrug, he turned away.

The two men sat across from each other, Ned on the bed, Liam, arms folded, on a low stool.

"You'll remember," Ned began, "how from the start I wanted you to admit the truth? Explain it was a friend who was writing the letters for you? And, later, when you offered to marry her, to admit it was only a joke about the promotion? But you kept putting me off?"

"Is this why you've asked me over here? To chew on that old shoe? What difference does it all make now? I have more important matters to think about. I turned down a chance to deliver a load of coal for Hennesy to come here."

Ned was reminded of himself as a boy, when his father had caught him out. As Ned talked, Liam gradually abandoned his defensive pose and began to stare intently at the wall above Ned's head. Even after Ned finished, the younger man had dropped his eyes to meet Ned's and continued to stare, as if waiting for him to continue. To add the necessary embellishment to make sense of this improbable story. When Ned failed to say anything else, Liam began to question him.

"Are you telling me she's quality? That I've married above my class? What do you take me for? You met her father."

"She knows all about you. Nora Flynn couldn't stop laughing when Anne claimed you were a foreman."

"Nora Flynn is a cheap whore," Liam muttered.

"You'd know about cheap whores, wouldn't you?"

Liam jumped to his feet and turned a furious face to Ned. "That's none of your business," he protested. His words had a quaver.

"The whole saloon knows about your visit to the American Hotel."

Liam sat back down on the stool. "Anne has... Anne found

out.... We can't have children, and it's my fault."

Now it was Ned's turn to be stunned. He was reluctant to pursue this, but could not resist asking, "What do you mean, your fault?"

"You remember. The night before the wedding, when the mates took me up the river to Diamond Street. I picked up something. Then I thought it had gone away."

"Dear God. Are you saying you have syphilis? That you gave syphilis to Anne?" Ned shuttered his face in his hands.

Liam had abandoned his posturing. His words were soft with remorse and confusion and his eyes began to fill.

"Everyone knows how hard I work. I've done everything I can think of to get ahead. To lift myself up. I married a decent girl, and find out she's not the girl I thought. Now, there's to be no baby, no family. The schooner—it was to get me on my way. On my own two feet. Am I to spend the rest of my days digging clay and heaving bricks? It wasn't to be like this. I was marked at birth for a charmed life." Liam touched his shirt and rubbed the place where the caul hung in its leather pouch. "I'm like a prisoner. I might as well stop chasing down ways to escape."

Ned sighed, "There was a time when I felt trapped as you do now. I wasted years in misery. Finally, I began to sift through my ideas, my notions about where I fit in the world. To decide where I was at fault, and what was beyond my control. What I stumbled on was honesty. While it's not always easy, there is no better way to live."

"What I'm saying," he continued, "is instead of letting Mr. Curran or anyone else make your decisions for you, instead of worrying about other people, always trying to earn their approval, find out who you are. If there's something about yourself that you don't like, then do something about it. Dare to admit the truth. And start with your wife."

26

Christmas with Liz and her family reminded Anne of Quebec. The table was spread with damask and crystal and gleaming china.

"Every Sunday, when Aiden, my husband, was alive, I put out the sterling and my best dishes to please him. 'Why keep it shut away in a cupboard?' he'd ask. 'What are you saving it for?' he'd say. As it turned out, he was right."

Liz unhurriedly fitted slender white candles into silver candelabra at each end of the table. Anne marveled at her serenity. There was neither bustle nor sign of anxiety as she tackled the multiple demands of the dinner. The children had been banished to the basement in the company of Ned and Liam, where the saloon served as their recreation room.

"How long has your husband been dead?" Anne asked, as she moved around the table, setting a folded linen napkin at each place.

"Robbie was a month old. He'll be six in February."

"You were left with an brand new infant?"

"Kate was one and Theresa three."

"How did you ever manage?"

"Friends, family, people from the church. All did what they could. But it was a horrid time. I don't know to this day how I kept from throwing myself off a cliff. I was a twenty-four-year-old

140

widow with three little ones to worry about, a big house on a hill, and no one to take care of me. So I realized I'd have to take care of myself. Sold the house, sold the schooners, lowered my sights, and landed here on Broad Street. Where I'm Liz. No more Mrs. Aiden Farrelly. And it's a good life. Come, let's get the rest of them upstairs so we can eat."

As soon as Liam came upstairs, Anne knew something was wrong. His speech was slurred, and he clutched at a chair back for support. He'd been drinking. She looked quickly at Ned who made a helpless gesture with his shoulders and hands.

"Mama, can I sit next to Ned?" Robbie pleaded.

"No, Mama, it's my turn," Kate protested.

"It will be neither of you," Liz answered. "Mrs. O'Connor is our guest, and she will sit at Ned's right hand, and Mr. O'Connor at his left."

"You make Ned sound like he's the king of England." Liam's voice trailed off.

Anne had not seen him this drunk since their wedding. She was torn between relief that she did not have to sit next to Liam nor speak to him, and concern that he was about to disrupt their festive meal. But, somehow, Ned kept him in check and he had little else to add. In fact he grew silent, making a few gestures at putting a forkful of food in his mouth, then slumping back in his chair, his eyes on his plate. Liz led the conversation, asking the children in turn to explain to Anne what they were studying in school. Theresa led the way with an elaborate description of her geography class.

"Geography is my favorite subject. Switzerland and Italy and France. I want to go there when I'm older."

"Have you studied about Canada?" Anne asked her.

Theresa thought for a moment. "Very little."

"I attended school in Canada, and taught there for a short while."

"Mama says you may be a teacher at St. Peter's."

"Yes, I will teach first grade when school resumes in January."

Liam, who had appeared almost comatose, stirred. Looked up, first at Anne, and then at Ned.

"What?" he asked, mystified. "What are you talking about?"

"I think it is time for the plum pudding," Liz announced. "Theresa, please help me clear the table."

Distracted, Liam became absorbed in the removal of plates and platters, then slumped back into his stupor. Anne saw the children share quick glances and suppressed grins. She felt a painful contraction in her stomach, and a tight ache in her throat.

"Oohs" and "ahs" erupted from the children. Anne looked up to see, held ceremoniously aloft, the plum pudding wreathed in blue flames. Then Liam collapsed against the table, his head sideways on the cloth. Robbie giggled and Liz hushed him. The boy clapped a hand across his mouth and lowered his head, but his body shook with laughter.

"I am so sorry… I am desperately sorry."

"It's nothing you need apologize for, pet. As my husband would say, 'it's a good man's failing.' Ned, go up to the stable on Broadway and hire a rig. Let's hope they haven't closed for Christmas."

As the three of them rode back to the boarding house, Ned confided that, while they kept out of the way before dinner, he and Liam were playing a guessing game with the children.

"The next thing I knew, he'd stepped behind the bar, announced it was time for a Christmas drink, and began helping himself to Liz's best whiskey. I didn't know what to do, being sort of the host. I tried to humor him, even asked him to pass the bottle to me, but he knows I'm no drinker. I could tell the children were taking it all in and I didn't want a row in front of them."

27

Liam agreed to accompany Anne on her traditional New Year's Day visit to her father and they caught an early morning train out of West Haverstraw.

Anne had found the wedding gift in an inside pocket of Liam's best suit and now it was in her purse. If only he had shown it to her, she could have told him it was not a deed. She waited until the train had pulled out of the station and was traveling along the bank of the Hudson River.

"Do you have any interest in farming the land up in Chestnut Grove?"

"None at all. Why would I break my back on a patch of land up there, when there is no guarantee that hail or drought or some sort of insect wouldn't, in a blink, wipe out everything, wasting not only my time but the money I'd have lost not working for a salary elsewhere. I'm not leaving Haverstraw."

"Nor do I have any wish to live in Chestnut Grove or to leave Haverstraw."

"What sensible woman would?"

"About the wedding gift. It's worthless to us. We can't sell it. We should give it back to my father."

"Give it back? It was a gift. It must have some value. To someone."

"My father had no savings that I know of. I'm sure he signed a note, and is slowly paying Mr. Lessard off."

"You're his daughter. He owed us a gift."

"And this was typical of him. Gave us what was really a gift to himself. I'm certain of that. He knew, with you working alongside him, he'd easily make enough to pay off the debt."

"Somehow, it doesn't seem right. I'm in no position to give anything away."

"Soon I'll be bringing home money."

She explained how the priest had offered her a job. That she'd be teaching at St. Peter's School. And still helping Nora with breakfast and dinner.

"After I've saved a bit, I hope we can move somewhere else, out of that attic. Find an inexpensive place where I can cook our own meals, and can sit in a chair at night and read a book."

"How much will they pay you?"

"I never asked. I was so excited just to be teaching again."

"You, a teacher." He shook his head. "At first, I was sure Ned had made it all up. To get back at me. But the more I thought about it, about you coming from money, I could believe it was true. But you had me fooled, you did."

"I've told you how sorry I am. I never considered how unfairly I was treating you."

"Well, you got the worst of the bargain."

"I can't permit you to think that. Look at how much better my life is, Liam, since I married you. I'm not buried alive on a farm in Chestnut Grove. I live in one of the most prosperous villages on the Hudson River, with a fine library, and every kind of shop. We're on the doorstep of New York City, where I hope you will take me someday."

His tone changed at the mention of Manhattan. "I'll take you there, gladly. Show you the sights. I was beginning to doubt myself, after all that's happened to me these last few weeks, but, with your help, the two of us, we can still get along."

Anne sighed quietly to herself. She could give back the gift.

When Anne pushed open the cabin door she found both her brothers, along with her father and Marie, Lessard's daughter, seated at the long kitchen table, chattering animatedly in French. Anne was struck by how stuffy the cabin grew with the door and windows closed and a meal cooking in the oven.

She and Liam were welcomed with loud greetings and waving arms and room was made for them at the table. Additional mugs filled with wine were set before them. The warmth of their reception seemed to dispell the stifling air.

Anne unwrapped the meat pies she had prepared earlier and room was found for them in the oven.

During the meal, as her father helped himself to a second serving, he said, "I miss your cooking. Marie is a hard worker. But not too good at baking." He winked at the young woman, who tossed her long hair.

Anne's older brother, Anton, was seated next to Marie. When he slipped his arm around her shoulders and laughingly drew her close to him, his father snarled at him.

"Behave yourself. After the plowing is done, Marie and I will marry."

Exclamations of astonishment were quickly followed with well wishes and laughter. Anne translated for Liam, "My father and Marie are to be married."

Marie lifted her chin and gave Anne a look that was both tentative and triumphant. She is barely sixteen, Anne thought. At last, her father has his alliance with Lessard. Little wonder he was so relaxed, so jubilant.

Anne helped Marie wash the dishes and pots while Liam and her brothers stepped outside the cabin to smoke their pipes. Her father, in his usual spot before the fire, sipped his wine.

When Anne handed her father the lease, she was properly apologetic and contrite. It was a most generous gift, but it was not possible for Liam to leave Haverstraw. Her father surprised her by accepting it back without comment. He'd probably done a quick calculation of the money he would save.

It was time for them to leave. Anne and her brothers knelt before their father to ask the traditional New Year's blessing. At first he teased that he might withhold it, but then placed his hand on each of their heads and invoked the benediction. Anne added a silent prayer of thanks that she was finally free of her father.

On the train ride back to Haverstraw, Liam, having drunk freely of the wine, as he had at his wedding the previous summer, fell asleep against the glass window of the railroad car.

Anne thought about the contents of a letter from Uncle Henri that had arrived the day before. He thanked her for her thoughtful greeting card and said it had brought momentary warmth into what had been the loneliest Christmas of his life.

He now realized what a mistake it had been to lease the house in Quebec. It held memories of the precious years of his marriage to Josie. He had decided to return to Quebec by March or April, and hoped Anne and her husband would join him. Make their home with him. She could help run the household and supervise the servants. He felt sure that suitable work could be found for Liam.

Anne's heart had leapt when she read the invitation. Quebec—beautiful Quebec—*rue Ste. Geneviève*....

But what about Liam? Uncle Henri could speak to people, find a position for Liam.

Just the thought of it. Of returning to Quebec. Did she dare allow herself to admit how intensely she missed the life she had known there? The shops, the entertainments. Would Celeste return also to keep house?

After Anne had discovered Liam's deception, it had been a struggle to reconcile herself to a lifetime with him, for there was no escaping the marriage, once she spoke her vows before a priest. With no reservations, she had fully committed herself to be his wife. Quebec might offer some reprieve from the consequences of her foolhardy choice.

In recent days, though, she found herself caring about what happened to Liam. She was able to see him apart from what had transpired between them.

She would have to overcome his reluctance to leave Haverstraw, present the move to Liam as a great opportunity for him. Emphasize the likelihood of a good salary, of advancement in a career. Uncle Henri had a wide circle of acquaintances, many of them successful businessmen.

An image intruded into her thoughts. Her father, with his two little sons clutching at his trousers, meeting her mother in the family kitchen, assuming she was a servant.

It would never work.

In Haverstraw Liam fit into a world that matched his background and abilities. Illiterate, unmannered, often crude, his friendships were with other men like him.

He showed no interest in learning to speak French. He spoke with her father through gestures, hand movements, and grunts.

No, there was no way her young Irish laborer could enter into the Quebec social life she had known before her marriage. Liam would be miserable in Canada.

28

Snow had been falling all day. The students were sent home early but Anne stayed behind to tidy her classroom and to prepare the following day's lesson.

Gales off the Hudson had whipped the snow into drifts. As she hurried through the swirling flakes, her arms crossed tightly against her chest for warmth, she passed a delivery wagon that stood sideways in the middle of Broadway. Its horse had slipped and fallen and was tangled in its harness. Two men assisted the driver as he struggled to right the beast.

When Anne finally reached the boarding house kitchen, tired but exhilarated by the season's first snowfall, she found Nora ironing.

"It reminds me of Quebec," Anne told her. "We had snow up there from October until May."

"They say this won't to stop before tomorrow. Thank heavens I have plenty of ham and potatoes. Enough to feed the men for days."

"Let me change my clothes so I can get started on the vegetables."

"Before you do that, tell me, how is the teaching?" Nora asked. "Is it still exciting, after five days?"

"It is a joy. Today, I taught the children some French words and they loved it."

"Well now, a French lesson. That's a new one for Haverstraw," Nora laughed. "I'll bet, when other parents hear about it, they'll want as much for their children."

"I stayed after school and drew a lesson on the blackboard. I outlined the shape of familiar objects, like a flower, a doll. Just simple things. Tomorrow, I'll make it a game: who can name the most objects."

"If you hadn't visited Father Grogan, you might be down on your knees up on Hudson Street, scrubbing some wealthy woman's floor. But wait, I have something to tell you.

"Curran's man was here today. He knocked on the door of every Curran property on Rockland Street and warned the tenants to find other lodgings. Said that last night a large crack opened down at the corner of Jefferson. As if people can just up and move. Where are they to go? You know how hard you've looked for a place."

"The yards have been closed down for two months, so there's no digging going on."

"Yes, but as soon as the river ice breaks up and the morning whistles sound, they'll be back on that clay bank like an army of ants. Mark my words. When the ground unfreezes, a house or two will go down. If you take a walk along the river and look westward, you can see the remains of houses that have fallen into the pit."

"When did Curran say he was moving this place?"

"He didn't. He'll have to give me a couple of days notice so I can put the men up somewhere else and get everything packed. If we keep having weather like today, I'd say perhaps late February, early March."

"I can't believe I won't find us our own place before that. Tomorrow, I'll ask the nuns. They must know of a family with a few extra rooms." The need to be settled in her own home had become a priority for Anne.

She would receive her first pay by the end of the week and prove to Liam they could afford to move.

Anne stepped out the back door to empty the trash, and stayed to enjoy the falling snow. It wove a silent cocoon over the neighborhood. Lamplight shone from the house next door and from a window across the way. Arc lamps that lined the sidewalk seemed to hang in mid-air, their posts obscured. A strong gust threw icy particles against her cheeks. She pulled her sweater snuggly around her and hurried back inside.

Nora had retreated to her room for the night. The remains of the dinner, in covered bowls, was stored in the pantry, and all pots and dishes in their proper places in cupboards. Anne decided to clean the glass chimney of the lamp that hung in the dining room. She spread rags and the long-handled brush on the kitchen table. She was tugging the glass from the fixture, when she heard movement and mumbled oaths coming from the kitchen.

It was Liam. His words were slurred and surly. "I'm the laughing stock of the saloon. Can't enjoy an evening with my mates anymore without having to listen to them. French! The lot of us can't even read English—and you've got their children talking French!"

He raised his fist and shook it at her.

Anne shrank back, anticipating a blow. Behind her the door cracked opened and Nora stormed out, her bathrobe half on, clutched across her broad midsection.

"What's this racket out here? What are you up to now, O'Connor? Look at you, falling all over yourself. Get up to bed with you. If I hear one more peep, I'll have you thrown out into the street."

Nora's boisterous manner and belligerent tone had their intended effect. Liam, cowed, headed for the stairs, and, without another word, began a stumbling ascent toward the attic.

"He was never a drinker," Nora lamented, "not like some of

them around here. He never gave me that problem before."

"I know. It's all my fault. I've ruined his life. Turned his friends against him."

"Don't go on like that. Women are always ready to take the blame for everything. You didn't ruin him. Why, he couldn't wait to show you off. To parade you around. The ninny. He has no idea what a treasure you really are. You're much too good for the likes of him."

"He's my husband."

Anne balanced her hip against the drain board of the sink as she rotated the brush inside the stained chimney. "I can't get it out of my thoughts, what's happening to Liam." She withdrew the brush and replaced it with crumpled newspaper which she twisted back and forth to loosen stubborn particles of soot. Her eyes on her task, she began to speak more slowly.

"Here I am teaching small children to speak French when maybe I should be teaching my husband to read, to write more than his name."

"He wouldn't stand still long enough," Nora countered.

"If I could get him past the shame."

Anne paused and turned her eyes upward as she rummaged through her thoughts.

"These past months have been topsy-turvy for me. I've stopped trying to make sense out of it all. He's different, the way he speaks to me. Ever since I told him about the doctor, things have changed. He leaves me alone now. And in the dining room, no one dares put a finger on me. Liam has no one, other than Ned and the men he works with. He really needs someone to look out for him. And I'm beginning to see he deserves my respect."

"Well, my girl, if you've made up your mind, God help him. He hasn't a prayer," Nora chuckled. "Good luck to you."

While Nora poured hot water into the teapot, Anne gave the lamp glass a final polish with a dry dishtowel and put it aside on the drain board. She pulled a chair from the table to join the older woman.

"It's so cold upstairs, I dread going up there. With him drunk, I want to be certain he's asleep before I climb into bed." She leaned forward, her forehead pressed against her palm, and shook her head.

Nora reached across and stroked her arm. "He'll be asleep before his head hits the pillow. Come on, pet, drink up while it's hot."

The women, each in her own thoughts, quietly sipped their steaming tea. From the window over the sink, Anne saw the soft pearl of a streetlight through the mist of tumbling flakes. The blanket of snow shrouding the neighborhood had wrapped the kitchen in its tranquil peace.

An ear-splitting, thunderous roar shattered the silence. The glass chimney tumbled from the sink and exploded across the linoleum.

Nora, her head poised like a sparrow's, listened for a moment, then leapt from her chair, grabbed Anne's arm and dragged her out the door. "Run!" she cried.

Alarmed, Anne, without waiting to don coat or boots, fled into the blackness, and then heard Nora call, "Wait! Anne! Take these little ones with you. Run for your lives! Head for the mountain. I have to rouse the men."

Two tiny faces with frightened eyes, mouths trembling, appeared through the swirling flakes. Shoeless, they hopped from one foot to the other, shivering in their flannel nightgowns. Anne quickly grasped a wrist of each and dragged them behind her. After a few steps, she stopped, took off her sweater and wrapped it around the taller of the two. She lifted the smaller child to her shoulder, clutched the hand of the other, and taking her bearing from the electric arc lights that lined the street, began to forge a path through the unplowed snow. Men and women stumbled out of houses. Every one screaming, running, some carrying lanterns. Children shrieking.

"Liz," she thought. "Which way is Liz's?"

Suddenly, from behind her, another grinding roar was followed by louder wailing. When she turned her head, it was as if a great lamp had been lit. Orange tongues of fire that rose high into the storm outlined rooftops, chimneys, and people carrying boxes, blankets, all heading toward her, past her, toward the mountain.

The terrified screams of the small child she carried urged her forward. "Hush, hush," she crooned. Anne no longer felt the cold. Felt only the hand of the older child that trustingly clutched hers and the weight of the small body she pressed against her breast.

Finally she reached Farrelly's, as Ned came hurrying down the shoveled path.

"Thank God, you're safe," he gasped.

He led her into the kitchen where Liz, her hair tumbled about her shoulders as if hastily pinned, took the child from Anne's arms and knelt and circled her arm around the other child. "You poor dears," she said softly, as she carefully wiped wet snow from their faces. "Not a shoe on either of you," she clucked. She eased the smaller child into a chair which she pulled close to the stove and drew another one near for the older child.

"Find a blanket for these waifs, while I make a pot of cocoa."

Liz turned to Anne who stood just inside the kitchen door. "It's the clay bank, isn't it? " Liz asked harshly.

When she received no reply, Liz looked more closely and saw, from Anne's lack of expression, that she had not been heard. Anne's eyes had the detached look of a sleepwalker.

Ned came out of his room with a blanket and tucked it around the two children.

"I must get down there and see how I can help." Without a glance at either woman, he left.

29

Buffeted by tearing winds, Ned struggled down Broad Street, his overshoes as much a hindrance as help as he navigated the drifted snow. At first he was guided through the darkness by a faint glow that filled the sky ahead of him, as well as the line of arc lamps along the north sidewalk, and the occasional lighted window. People bumped into him as they hurried in the opposite direction. The wailing of children mingled with older voices pleading for God's help. Ferocious gusts from the river plastered soot and snow against his lips, drove it up his nostrils. He pulled the brim of his hat down almost to the bridge of his nose to shield his eyes. When Ned rounded the corner from Broad into Rockland Street, the blackness disappeared into a monstrous, blazing furnace.

When, in the past, he had pictured the rim of the clay bank collapsing, he had not anticipated fire. Terrible devastation, but never fire. Yet, there had to be fire. Furnaces had been stoked with extra coal to carry through the long January night. Kerosene-filled lamps in every room. In some homes, gas lines.

In silhouette, panicked fire horses reared back from the blaze. Ned wondered which house, which houses, had fallen into the pit? Some on Rockland Street, that was certain. But the conflagration covered an enormous area. Part of Division Street? Liberty Street? Ten, maybe fifteen, buildings were lost.

Milling shadows flickered throughout the gathered throng. Ned thought he recognized men from the saloon and moved toward them. Liam was not among them.

"Someone get word to Garnerville." Tim Maloney's voice was hoarse from shouting directions. "We need their steam pumper. The hydrants are useless; the mains are broken."

"There's a telephone in the American Hotel."

A posse of onlookers took off toward Main Street.

Ned stared at the inferno before him. Was this the hell he had been raised to fear? The terrible punishment exacted for wrong-doing, for sinfulness? He shuddered when his ears caught faint voices from the cauldron, pleading, imploring God's help.

Sacred phrases from his former training sprang to Ned's mind. Prayers for the dying, for the dead. He stepped to the edge of the pit, his hands outstretched, and began to quietly intone the prayer, "Receive, O Lord, Thy servants into the place of salvation, which they hope to obtain through Thy mercy. Deliver them...." He was interrupted when a burly arm circled his waist and pulled him backward.

"Careful, mate. There could be another slide. Four firemen just vanished before our eyes, there one second, gone the next."

Shaken, Ned turned and saw Jack Reilly. "Jack, tell me, how can I help?"

"Go after the children. Find them shelter."

Children? Yes, he could do that. Ned turned from the pit, craned his head and listened. Amid the frenzied screams and bellowing voices, and over the roar of combusting wood, he identified the insistent squalling of an infant. He found it lying on a snow bank behind a hedge and quickly gathered it in his arms. Further along, beneath the hedge, a small boy was hunched against the whipping winds. Ned grabbed the boy's hand and pulled him close. When he found two slightly older children huddled under a blanket for a shield against the swirling snow, he led them, barefooted, stumbling, shivering, and bawling for their mothers, to St. Peter's School where he delivered them into the care of the waiting nuns.

Church bells throughout the village had begun to toll. As Ned hurried back to the site of the catastrophe, the air was thick with particles of wet soot. An acrid stench of burning paint and oil mingled with a horrid sweet smell that he feared was roasting flesh. He vomited.

At the aborted foot of Liberty Street, undeterred by the threat of sliding clay, a group of men were clustered. Some held lanterns above their heads.

Ned spoke to one on the edge of the group who explained. "Mrs. Gillespie is trapped down there. Her leg is pinned under the debris of the house. Her husband is inside, trying to free her."

Ned peered past the shoulders of the men in front of him and caught a glimpse of a woman's tormented face. Her mouth was stretched wide in a grimace of pain.

Flames had begun to consume several branches of a tree close by.

Suddenly a young man with a crowbar pushed his way through the group. He had tethered one end of a rope to a thick tree trunk and fastened the other end around his middle. He rappelled down to the trapped woman and after several tries, freed her leg, then grasping her under the arms, called for the men to pull them up. He had just handed the woman over and turned back for the husband, when the house, with a groan, slid into the darkness. An explosion, then a crackling burst of flame drove the onlookers back.

"Gas," one of the men commented. "Gas," several agreed.

The rescuer's pants legs had caught fire. As soon as he was pulled back up, he was eased to the ground and several of the men fell across him to smother the flames.

The woman had fainted. She lay on the back of a wagon, bundled in a quilt. The young hero, despite his protestations, was placed beside her and the driver turned the horses south toward the hospital in Nyack. A blanket of white quickly covered them.

"The snow is a blessing," someone said. "With all these frame houses and that wind blowing off the river."

"The entire village could have been lost. Thank God for the snow," other voices agreed.

Rough estimates of loss were being calculated. Ten buildings. Twenty, easily. Not more than fifteen.

In despair, Ned turned away to listen for a child's weeping, to comb the dark night for small huddled bodies. The snow now was falling in thick, pelting sheets.

When he suspected there were no more children to rescue, or at least none he could detect in the darkness, he abandoned his efforts. His legs ached from clambering over uneven piles of snow, his bare hands, for he had given his gloves to a young boy, were numb from the cold. He needed to find the sanity and sanctuary of Liz's kitchen.

30

It was Sunday. The church bells, which had began their slow tolling Monday midnight and continued throughout Tuesday, bearing a mournful witness to lost lives, now called the survivors to worship. Six days had passed since what was now called "the landslide." A shroud of ash still hung over the village. Everything, every place, every streetlight, storefront, every wagon, was covered with clotted soot. The snow had hardened in waist-high banks along rutted streets.

It was too cold to wash grime from windows and doors, so oil lamps burned throughout the day. A sense of stunned betrayal seemed to have paralyzed the village. When people spoke, they did not complete their sentences.

The mayor called a meeting at the Waldron Opera House on Tuesday night. A considerable sum of money was collected, and was handed over to the ladies at the King's Daughters Library for distribution. Families opened their homes to make room for survivors, most of whom were the children of parents who had carried them to safety before returning to collect valuables, losing their lives in the process.

Anne found it difficult to speak. To summon the will to frame words. The nuns gave her a bed at the convent, and she took charge of the children who'd been delivered into their care. She would smile at the children, hug them, and they accepted her silence. When the distraction of companions and play failed, and memories of abandonment overwhelmed them, she held the children, rocked them, and smoothed tears from their small cheeks. School had been cancelled indefinitely, as energies were refocused on adapting to this new universe of disrupted lives. Attempts began to locate relatives, to find living quarters, and resolve the inevitable disputes.

The Hot Air Society, nevertheless, held its annual dinner at the American Hotel and, according to *The New York Times*, had the largest attendance ever. The brickyard owners projected that the demand for brick would continue to rise along with the price.

A growing irritation for the villagers was the horde of curious who, by train and boat, arrived within days of the calamity. Rude and intrusive newspapermen assaulted whomever they met with a barrage of inquiries. Only that morning, Anne had answered the doorbell at the convent. A man stood on the doorstep and, anticipating a worried relative, she was about to invite him inside, when he began to pelt her with questions.

"How did it feel when the earth quiv…?"

Anne quickly shoved him back outside, slammed and locked the door. What has happened, she asked herself. What will happen? To these children? To Haverstraw? Questions swam about in her mind, shifted, overlapped. Where is Liam? She finally dared wonder. If he had perished, she was no longer bound to him. The unsuitability of such a thought, at a time when she should be grieving, astonished and shamed her. What about Nora, who'd dragged her out of the building and urged her to run toward the mountain? Was she alive? Nora. At the thought that Nora might be dead an emptiness began to swell inside her. Ned would know. Where was Ned?

Each morning on his way to help recover the bodies, he stopped at the kitchen door of the convent and asked how she was doing. Anne could barely reply, only a nod or a shrug. He never pressed for more. Perhaps by tomorrow she could ask him about Nora. And ask about Liam.

Here and there throughout the disaster area, small fires still burned. Ned clawed his way carefully through the charred timbers, aware that certain ones, when dislodged, often rekindled into flame. There was no careless talk in the pit as the corps of volunteers dug and pried their way through the chaos. Each one intent on a shared commitment to remove every corpse from this premature grave.

On last Tuesday morning, the recovery efforts had been postponed until the Quartermaster Corp from West Point could evaluate six structures that teetered at the edge of the pit. On their recommendation, all were razed, bringing the total number of homes and stores lost to the landslide to fifteen. The known number of dead was nineteen. Tramps often found shelter in backyard sheds and outbuildings; the death toll could be higher.

Ned was close by when Liam was found. It was as if his body had been hurled free of the flames when the boarding house collapsed, then smothered under a great wave of clay and sand. Untouched by the fire, his expression showed no awareness of his impending death. The leather pouch, his caul, hung from his neck.

Nora had not been as fortunate. Her robe was charred, her hair singed, her mouth frozen in an agonized scream. As the crew combed through the rubble for additional bodies, their shovels struck a solid object. They suspected at first that it was part of the foundation but it was a trunk. They hauled it up the clay bank and left it by the side of the road and returned to their grim task.

Several hours passed before Ned realized that the trunk resembled the one he and Liam had brought down from Chestnut Grove after the wedding and carried into the boarding house. When darkness began to close in and the recovery work was suspended, Ned stopped to check whether the leather handle on the left side was torn off. This was Anne's trunk. Soaked, stained, reeking of the smell of charred wood.

Ned found Anne in the convent kitchen, her arms deep in a pan of sudsy water, scrubbing the large pots and pans from supper.

She stared at Ned, as if trying to decipher the message he had delivered.

"Are you sure? It's my trunk?" The words flowed easily. She covered her mouth with her hand, as if she had spoken out of turn, and then smiled in relief. Her face came alive and Ned felt his heart expand inside him.

Then a grave look returned to her face. "What about Liam? Is there any news of Liam?"

Ned told her that her husband apparently had not awakened before he died. Handing her the small leather pouch, he explained, "I thought you might want to keep this. It may have saved him from the flames."

"No, that should be buried with him." Anne said. She shook her head. She hesitated and Ned saw pain enter her eyes. "Is there any news of Nora?" she asked anxiously.

Ned knew the truth would be hard for Anne to hear. But he had made a resolution; he would never deceive anyone ever again.

"Nora was not as fortunate as Liam," he said softly.

Anne burst into tears and crumpled against his shoulder. She clung to him briefly, then composed herself and blew her nose on a square of cambric she had tucked up her sleeve.

"She was the dearest, the truest friend. She took me under her wing from the first moment we met. I could talk to her, I could tell her anything. Oh, I will miss her. I will miss her so."

Ned compared her calm acceptance of her husband's passing with her passionate response to Nora's death. But he understood.

The realization that Anne was no longer a married woman swept across his mind. Elation was quickly followed by reproach and he felt the heat of shame warm his face. What sort of man had such thoughts about a woman who was widowed less than a week?

He bowed his head to hide his flushed cheeks and he cleared his throat. "They took the bodies up to Shankey's Funeral Home where a morgue has been set up. I hope you'll let me handle the details of both funerals. Please."

"Nora has a niece down in Nyack. She must be frantic."

"I'll find her," Ned assured Anne. "I have your trunk outside on a cart. Would you'd like me to store it over at Liz's?"

"That would be good. And thank you. For all you've done."

Ned did not climb up onto the wagon but instead walked alongside the horse, guiding it down the dark, icy roads toward Broad Street. The weariness and fatigue from the hours spent on the smoldering pile of rubble had evaporated, replaced by the memory of Anne's head pressed against his shoulder.

31

When Ned saw a sign indicating the entrance to the Sparkill School for Boys, he pulled on the left rein to guide the horse toward the circular drive that fronted the tall brick building. Seated next to him in the carriage, Anne removed her hat to tuck back stray locks that had come loose on the trip from Haverstraw. Satisfied, she returned the gray chinchilla hat to her head and secured it with a long, pearl-tipped pin. She brushed the skirt of her navy traveling suit with her hand and lifted the matching fur muff into her lap.

"Which order did you say this is?"

"Dominicans. They moved their motherhouse up from Manhattan when the orphanage was rebuilt. After the fire."

"I hope they're not stern. And that they won't make me feel ten years old."

"You surprise me when I hear you say such things."

Anne was sure that the timid young woman who answered the door was a postulant, because her hair was only partly hidden by a veil. She opened a highly varnished double door and led them into a parlor.

"Please be seated. The Reverend Mother will be with you shortly."

The room was beautifully furnished, with an oriental rug covering the floor and cut glass lamps on small tables. Anne selected a side chair covered in maroon velvet, that matched the sofa with a carved wood frame on which Ned sat.

As they each were exploring and commenting on the contents of the room, another double door across from the one they had entered opened and a heavy-set nun approached them, her hand extended in a greeting, a cordial smile on her face

"He was a rascal, that Liam," the nun confided. "He could charm a cat. We had no choice but to put him in with the small ones when we found out he could neither read nor write. The big lads made much of it. He fought right back. Wouldn't hesitate to take on the largest ones, even when he knew he'd be beaten.

"When he found out the older boys were going up to Rockland Lake to cut ice, he wouldn't let up. He wanted the money. It was a nine-mile walk each way, but that was nothing to him."

"We sent a letter to Father Frank, after Liam ran away. We received a letter months later saying the mother had been sent back to Connamara, half out of her mind at losing Liam. I have his address somewhere around here, if you'd like it."

"That would be very kind of you," Anne said. "I think Liam's family should be told of his death."

Anne's efforts to locate someone who cared for Liam was largely motivated by guilt over her lack of remorse. It seemed only right that somebody should mourn him.

On the carriage ride back to Haverstraw, Anne turned to Ned.

"You know all about me and I know next to nothing about you."

"There isn't much to tell," he answered. Then he remembered his pledge to never deceive her again. Did he dare tell her the truth?

They rode along in silence for several minutes. Then Ned began, haltingly, to share his past.

"Back in Ireland, when I was fifteen, I entered the novitiate and later the seminary. Those were the most wonderful years of my life. It was my intention to completely surrender my life to God and His will for me. From the day I made that decision, I hadn't a moment of doubt. The months quickly became years and, finally, I was about to be ordained."

Fascinated, Anne could not take her eyes off him. The words were pouring out in a torrent, yet he spoke quietly. Now and then, he would snap the reins to remind the horse to keep pace.

"The week before the ceremony was to take place, the rector called me into his office. He said I was not to be ordained and I was to leave the seminary at once. Despite all my training in obedience, I pleaded for an explanation.

"There was never an explanation. To this day, I have no idea why I was dismissed. My spiritual director, with whom I had conferred throughout my seminary experience, could not understand. He urged me to persist. To write to the head of the order, and when no response came from him, finally to Rome. Again, I received no reply. A month passed. I was now shunned by the members of my community and finally I was told I must leave the grounds the following morning. A carriage would take me to the train station. I was given the black suit I was to wear following my ordination and a five-pound note."

"How unfair, how unbearably cruel."

"Yes, it was cruel. More so for my mother who had regaled her neighbors with her plans. She was to travel to Belfast with my father and share my special day. Can you imagine the agony of having to tell her to not come? I couldn't trust the post. I took the train from Belfast to my hometown and I'll never forget the struggle on her face to comprehend my news. She insisted there had been a mistake, hugged me and assured me that it would all work out. I never doubted she'd believe me, accept me, but she had waited all those years for my first blessing, the entitlement of every priest's mother."

"How did you ever get over it?"

"It took me a very long time. You must know there is no one more scorned than a failed priest."

"But you were never a priest," Anne protested.

"People do not draw such fine lines. Not even my father. Mortified in front of his neighbors, he gave my mother some money, told her to give it to me and to tell me to leave. Said I knew full well why I was thrown out, but I was too much of a coward to admit it. He had overheard a man in the local pub say as much."

"You don't have to tell me any more. I had no idea...."

"You are the only person, aside from my family in Ireland, who knows about this. Can you imagine how Haverstraw would react if they heard I'd left the seminary? No different than that man in my father's pub. I'm grateful to you for listening."

The road curved for several hundred yards until, in front of the carriage, the wide expanse of Haverstraw Bay was spread out before them. Anne caught her breath, as always, at the view. From the road, which was midway up the side of the Palisades, they looked out over the village, over the bare branches of the trees and the brickyard sheds, and across the placid water to the eastern shore of the river.

Anne never tired of the sight. For some reason, she had failed to notice it when their carriage passed on the way down to Sparkill earlier in the day. Then she remembered what had preoccupied her, what distracted her, and she smiled at the memory.

After early Mass at St. Peter's, she had walked over to Liz's for a quick breakfast, while Ned stopped by the stable to pick up a rig. It was a cloudless, sunny day, unusually warm for February, and there was little need to turn collars up against the wind and cold. He had just helped her up into the carriage and, as he was arranging the heavy lap robe around her knees, she noticed at the nape of his neck, a wave of small curls. As she might, had it been a child, Anne was inclined to lean down and stroke it. She had to shake her head to clear away the image.

Ned was a good friend, on whom she had come to depend in so many ways. He had spared her the details of the funeral and burial. And he brought her to McCann's office to begin legal proceedings to settle what was absurdly referred to as Liam's estate. She did not know why, but the nape of Ned's neck both fascinated and unsettled her. She began to speculate on his relationship with Liz. They were obviously very fond of each other.

Her thoughts had wandered and she had failed to notice the river until it appeared before them, welcoming them back to Haverstraw. In the aftermath of the landslide, caught up in finding homes for the orphans and searching for their relatives, Anne had forgotten about the river. Today it flowed by, majestically, silent, composed.

Ned noticed her look and asked, "Did you know it's a tidal estuary of the Atlantic Ocean more than it is a river? When the tide comes in, it brings salty sea water all the way up to Poughkeepsie, miles north of here."

"I'm afraid my education was limited. There have been times when I feel close to the river. That it is my protector." She looked quickly, to see his reaction. He was nodding in agreement so she continued.

"Up in the boarding house attic, when I was really desperate, I used to talk to the river. I thought it answered me. Does that sound strange to you?"

"No."

Ned understood. He didn't mock or chide her. She should have known he wouldn't. How different Ned was from Liam, from her father, her brothers. Would Paul understand? Paul seemed to think everything about her was perfect but, that was not the same as understanding. Paul had no idea who she was, really, while Ned knew everything about her. Well, almost everything. Wondering about Paul led her mind to Uncle Henri.

"A day or so after Christmas a letter arrived from my uncle, Aunt Josie's husband. I came across it yesterday while I was looking in my trunk."

"He was very good to you, wasn't he?"

"Yes, he was. In his letter, he suggested that Liam and I come live with him in Quebec."

"I thought he'd moved to Toronto."

"He did, but he sees now it was a mistake to leave *rue Ste. Geneviève*. His fondest memories are there, as are mine."

"Are you are going to go back?" His question seemed cautious, as if he did not approve such a decision.

"At least for a short visit. I want to see him, and, more than that, I need to find out if I'm ready to manage my uncle's home and help him entertain. There was a time when the idea would have thrilled me, but I'm a different person now. I'm not sure I could give up teaching."

"You taught in Quebec."

Anne sighed.

"There are some things about myself I haven't told you. I can assure you, my teaching days in Quebec are finished, with the nuns at least."

Ned and Liz drove Anne to the train station at West Haverstraw. Liz chattered on about the box lunch she had packed and how she was looking forward to Anne's letters. Ned, his heart heavy, found it difficult to talk. He was determined to be pleasant, but his manner had turned brusque.

"You seem angry at me. Have I said something to offend you?" Anne placed her hand on his arm and looked into his eyes. They were clouded, and could not hold her gaze.

"It's just—it's just that…" he stammered.

"He doesn't want you to go," Liz interrupted, "any more than I do. You know how much we care about you. It's hard to say goodbye. I'm a bit better at it than Ned."

Liz's words broke the tension and Anne smiled at both of them.

"A part of me wishes I weren't leaving. But the rest of me can't wait to see Uncle Henri again. I'll send postcards to you and the children so you can see how lovely Quebec's gardens and parks are."

With the help of a porter, Ned lifted Anne's battered trunk into the baggage car, recalling the night he and Liam had unloaded it onto this very platform. *For everything there is a season and a time....* He took oblique comfort from *Ecclesiastes*.

A week later, an envelope addressed to him lay on the kitchen table. Ned pounced on it, assuming it was from Anne. Inside, he found a note from the head of the orphanage in Sparkill. The Mother Superior was offering him a job supervising the older boys. He knew it was time for him to move on. He no longer had to hide behind a grocery counter or a bar. His wounds had been licked long enough.

Soon he was living in a dormitory again, although more lively and noisier than the ones at the seminary.

Whenever a letter from Anne arrived, he reread it several times, then, as soon as the children had settled down for the night, he composed an answer. Before breakfast, the next day, he walked into town and delivered it to the local post office, in hopes it would hasten a reply.

The boys took to him at once. They decided he was a friend and sought him out for companionship and comfort. He sat with them in the dining hall and joined in their conversations and he impressed them with his ability to score goals on the soccer field. His sense of loss gradually lessened, though a quiet ache remained.

The months passed and then, finally, one morning he woke and knew he was happy. He was content. The night before, as he was falling asleep, he'd realized he had failed to check his mail, preoccupied by the day-to-day tasks the supervision of children entail. Ned had reached another turning point in his life.

32

Several weeks had passed since Anne returned to Quebec. She lay one morning, reluctant to leave her comfortable bed, and allowed her thoughts drift. Uncle Henri's warm concern and Celeste's devoted cosseting had restored her sense of well-being. Still, a vague restlessness stirred at the edge of her contentment. She was becoming impatient for something new to happen.

Outside her window, there were sounds of scratching and fluttering. She rose, looked out and saw a sparrow with a piece of straw in its beak disappear up into the eaves. A moment later it flew off. She continued to watch the small bird carrying small bits of straw. Later she planned to go outside and look for the nest.

While she rummaged through her closet for a suitable outfit her eye fell on a pale blue skirt that needed to be hemmed. Celeste would help her pin it up.

After breakfast, Anne, wearing the skirt, stood on a kitchen chair. Celeste knelt on the floor fastening the fabric. Periodically, through lips that held straight pins, she'd grunt a signal for Anne to rotate slightly.

"Where is that pincushion I bought you? With the elastic strap for your wrist? Some day you'll swallow a pin," Anne playfully chided her.

Celeste shook her head, then removed the remaining pins from her mouth. She leaned on the chair for support as she lifted herself up. "There. I'll iron the crease and you can stitch it."

Anne stepped down from the chair. "Thank you again. You do everything for me. Sometimes I forget I worked in a boarding house."

"I'm happiest when I'm busy. Your uncle is rarely home, and there is only so much work for one person."

"This morning I watched a sparrow build a nest and I felt lazy."

Celeste reached under the sink, pulled out two irons and set them on the stove to heat while Anne retrieved a padded board that was stored behind the pantry door. From a cupboard Celeste removed a colorful straw box, which she handed to Anne. "I'm sure you'll find light blue thread in here."

Anne pulled the chair she had been standing on over to the kitchen table. From Celeste's sewing basket she selected a needle and began to thread it.

"Did you like either of those young men your uncle invited to dinner?" Celeste asked.

"I doubt I will remarry," Anne said.

"How can you say that? There are hundreds of suitors for an attractive woman like you. Wealthy ones, too. You must give them a chance."

"I cannot bear a child." She was surprised how calmly she said it.

Celeste stared at her. "How can that be?"

Anne's voice quavered. "My husband was not clean. Now, I am not clean."

She felt the tears begin to spill down her face. "A doctor warned me my child could be born blind, or worse."

Celeste insisted Anne make an appointment with Doctor Robichaud, and several days later accompanied her to his enormous gray stone house on the other side of town. An oriental rug covered the floor of the waiting room and a slim vase held a spray of crisp white tulips. Dr. Robichaud greeted Anne warmly and, after being introduced to Celeste, agreed that she could participate in the visit.

Anne knew he was putting her at her ease by reminiscing about her aunt and inquiring about the health of her uncle. "Such a devoted couple. He must be lost without her." Then his tone turned sober. "Tell me why you have come?"

Celeste held her hand during the examination and later helped her back into her clothes. When they returned to the doctor's office they found him at his desk, his head bent over the page before him, the nib of his pen scratching furiously across it.

He looked up at Anne and his face revealed nothing.

It is worse than I thought, she told herself.

When he spoke, it was with modulated rage. "The man is a fool. How he could have mistaken a common feminine malady for an incurable disease is beyond comprehension. How he could have examined you and come to such a...."

Anne interrupted him. "He never examined me."

The doctor glared at her. "Never examined you? Then how did he make a diagnosis?"

"He heard me speak with a French accent. I described my discharge and my discomfort. 'You French gals,' he said with contempt. I protested that I was married. Then he said it would be dangerous to conceive a child."

"Did he prescribe arsenic?" She detected a hint of worry in his question.

"He prescribed nothing. He wanted me to leave."

On the carriage ride home, Celeste held her hand. Neither woman spoke. The only sounds were horse's hooves clattering across cobblestones. Anne felt neither joy nor exhilaration. Rather a guilty sense of freedom. The last shreds of her life as Liam's wife were unraveling.

The following morning lying in bed, she listened to the rustling outside her window. The birds are about their business, she thought. What was her business?

Should she consider marriage? In view of her widowed state, her age, and her lack of inheritance, the field would be narrow. The likelihood uncertain.

What about Paul?

Anne waited impatiently on the striped settee, feigning interest in her uncle's conversation with Madam Vallon while she listened for the doorbell. Earlier that week Anne had stopped at the bookstore to determine whether Paul still worked there. She pushed open the door and heard the crowded shop buzzing with excited chatter. Paul was at the cash register. She felt her heart rise into her throat. Two women, waving books, vied for his attention. It was no time for a visit. He looked older, heavier, his hairline had receded. When she finally caught his eye, it was obvious he did not know who she was.

"Can I help…?" and then he recognized her. "Such a delightful surprise." He lifted his shoulders in a gesture of helplessness. "It is frantic today."

She reached for a blank sales slip, quickly wrote her address and handed it to him with a note inviting him to lunch the following Sunday.

He nodded as another book was thrust at him.

As she walked back toward the funicular at the Frontenac stairway her composure returned. Instead of boarding the inclined cable car, she decided to climb the long flight of steps. The exercise would do her good. He did not recognize her. Then said she was a delightful surprise.

She heard the sharp ring of the bell. Then the patter of Celeste's footsteps, and through the arched doorway that opened into the front hallway, saw a flash of her white apron. Her heart began to pound and she held her breath for a moment.

The housekeeper came into the parlor, approached Anne and murmured that Monsieur Vasseau had arrived. Uncle Henri and his companion had looked up when Celeste entered the room and now watched Anne expectantly.

"As I told you at breakfast, Uncle, I am spending the afternoon with Paul but I will be back for dinner." As she spoke, she rose to leave, crossing over to her uncle to kiss him. She curtseyed to Madame Vallon, but did not escape so easily, for her uncle insisted on being introduced to her friend.

"Ah, Paul. Yes, I remember. You came to dinner several years ago, when my wife was still alive."

"I am sorry to learn of your loss, Monsieur Pelletier, and offer you my most sincere condolences. That dinner has been a most pleasant memory."

Madame Vallon nodded politely when introduced, but Anne caught a flicker of appraisal in her glance, a question.

When Anne first mentioned her plans to Uncle Henri, he did not recall having met Paul. Nonetheless, when she explained that they would be going out for lunch, he'd insisted she call the Chateau Frontenac and make a reservation in his name. Anne had hoped he would say that.

Paul seemed bewildered when she led him back to the front door. "We have reservations for lunch at the Frontenac," she explained. "We have so much to talk about. It would have been awkward here, with my uncle and Madame Vallon."

They were descending the front steps when he began to stammer, and then laughed. It was Anne's turn to be puzzled.

"I'm sorry—so elegant a restaurant. I had expected…."

She raised her palm to hush him. "Please. It is my uncle's treat."

Paul drew a deep breath, exhaled, and turned to face her. "Forgive my confusion. You've appeared out of the blue after so long a time." He drew another deep breath and sighed.

Anne was perplexed as well. She had anticipated a light-hearted reunion. A bit of the excitement she'd felt that day in the Beaupré cafe where they'd laughed with the other pilgrims. Perhaps locking arms as they had that sunny afternoon on the Dufferin terrace. Instinctively she drew back. She was not the young girl who had dashed off to New York. Any more than he was the man she'd imagined lay with her instead of Liam. She cringed at the memory of her daydreams.

"Come, let's take the path through the park," she suggested.

A murmur of hushed voices filled the dining room, every table seemed occupied. Anne was pleased where they were seated. At a table next to the large window that overlooked the small park they had walked through, where over brilliant green lawns, baskets filled with deep blue lobelia, ivy, and pink petunias hung from the lamp posts.

"I'm certain they saved this particular table for my uncle. He often brings his lady friends here."

After they gave their selections to the waiter, there was a brief, strained silence. Anne began to speak of her marriage, and the tragic accident that killed her husband. Paul interrupted, as if he had barely heard her, and began to explain why his funds were so limited.

"My former wife died in childbirth last winter. Her husband wrote to tell me that my daughter misses her dreadfully. Emilie cries all the time. I'm going to bring her back here."

He went on the explain how expensive such a trip would be. It meant many weeks without a salary. He would have to pay his rent in advance. When Anne brought up her experiences in New York, he turned the conversation back to his difficult circumstances. He was a stranger. Or was she the stranger? In desperation, she inquired about his favorite authors. Could he recommend any new and interesting writers?

"I sell books," he explained patiently. "I catalog them, shelve them, recommend them to customers. I don't read them."

Shocked, but unwilling to reveal it, she commented on the excellence of the wine the steward had recommended. She let her eyes wander outside to the park where clusters of families strolled the paths, children chasing each other across the grass.

They finished lunch and Anne made an excuse of having to be home early. When they parted at the foot of the steps of her uncle's house, Paul leaned to kiss her and she took a step back. He asked if she would like to visit the *Quartier Petit-Champlain* the following Sunday. Uncertain, she agreed.

Because it was the Sabbath, none of the businesses, other than restaurants, along the narrow cobblestone streets were open. At a local *patisserie* they ate *petits fours* with their *demitasse*, and Anne thought about the napoleon she'd intended to buy at Mardof's bakery in Haverstraw. She remembered when she visited the secondhand store and priced the table with the chipped veneer. That same table, along with the entire contents of that store, may have slid down the embankment to be consumed by the inferno.

Madame Vallon's visits to *rue Ste. Geneviève* had become an almost daily occurrence and Anne realized she would not want to live there if her uncle remarried.

When Paul said goodbye that afternoon, she told him she would not be seeing him again because she was returning to Haverstraw.

If he was disappointed, he concealed it well. "You come into my life from out of the past, and now you are to disappear once more." She let him kiss her cheek before turning away. When Anne reached the top of the steps, rang the bell and looked over her shoulder, he had not moved. He continued to stand there, staring at her as she entered the house.

She was surprised to hear herself say she was returning to New York, but the idea had been forming for some days. The announcement of her decision resolved any lingering doubts.

33

Sunday was Ned's day off. He faithfully rode the train up to Haverstraw for dinner with Liz and the children, and caught up with the events of the past week. It was on such a Sunday, toward the end of October, that he opened the back door into kitchen and found Anne standing at the sink alongside Liz.

For a moment he hesitated, "When did you ..." before he rushed over, wrapped his arms around Anne, lifted her off the floor, swinging her around and around. The three children, who had been playing on the floor, jumped up and began to leap about with cries of "We fooled you, Ned! We fooled you!"

Liz, briefly wreathed in steam from hot liquid she had poured into the sink, put the drained pot aside and turned to shush the children. Ned released a flustered Anne and, slightly abashed, turned a bewildered, questioning face to Liz, who rescued the situation by announcing that dinner would be served as soon as the potatoes were mashed.

"Theresa, Kate, Robbie, hands washed at once." The children ran off and left Anne and Ned to grin at each other.

"My word. That was the most exuberant welcome I've ever received. My grandfather used to swing me about like that when I was a little girl."

"I couldn't help myself," Ned apologized. "You were the last person I expected to find here."

Anne smiled at him.

"I know you'll forgive me for keeping you in the dark, Ned. I wasn't sure exactly when I would arrive."

"She turned up on our doorstep last night, chipper as a bird." Liz said laughing.

"Just like that—she turned up?"

Anne found an apron hanging with the coats beside the back door.

"Here, let me earn my keep."

Anne pulled the pot of potatoes to the front of the stove, and began to break them up with a wire masher. She added the heated milk and butter Liz had prepared in a small pan, threw in a handful of salt, fluffed them with fork, put a lid on the finished potatoes and returned them to the rear of the stovetop to keep warm. Talking while she worked, Anne explained that she had written to Liz a month earlier.

"I asked if she could put me up for a short while until I can get resettled. She told me I could have your old room."

"Resettled," Ned repeated.

"Quebec was lovely and Uncle Henri is a dear, but he has scads of widows dying to have him over for dinner and to accompany him to the opera and concerts. One in particular seems to have caught his fancy."

"But you…?"

"I'm not a genteel lady in a silk dress. I grew up in a mill town in Maine. As rough as Haverstraw but not as exciting. After a month or so in my uncle's home, I began to feel as if I were an actress in a play. Haverstraw is real. I want to see New York City. I want to see everything!"

Ned was so lightheaded he doubted that his feet were touching the ground. Robbie appeared from nowhere and clutched his legs. "Swirl me around like you did Mrs. O'Connor," he begged.

"I'll swirl you. Right into your chair," and Ned plunked the child down alongside Anne. He avoided her eyes, not trusting what his might reveal.

After the dinner dishes were done, Anne offered to help the children with their lessons for the next day. Quickly the four gathered around the kitchen table, each youngster vying for Anne's attention

"Come, let's get some fresh air in our lungs," Liz said to Ned.

The late afternoon was clear and cool, cool enough for sweaters. The sun had begun to drop behind the Tor, and the bare trees raised black branches against the twilight sky. Fallen leaves, in shades of gold and red, covered the brick sidewalks and lawns.

Liz took Ned's arm in hers. "When are you going to ask Anne to marry you?"

"Are you mad?" he sputtered.

"You'd like to marry her, wouldn't you?" She asked it kindly, gently, telling him more than inquiring.

"Her husband's hardly cold in his grave."

"It was not a match made in heaven."

"Why would a lovely woman like Anne want to marry the likes of me?" His voice cracked as he completed the question.

"You'll never know unless you ask her."

Ned floundered for words. "It's... preposterous. Why, it's ludicrous...absurd...."

"You are a good man. I don't understand why you think so poorly of yourself."

Ned pulled a watch from his trousers. "Look at the time, Liz. I'll have to hurry if I'm to catch the train back to Sparkill."

As the train pulled away from Haverstraw, Ned's mind was aflame. Liz didn't understand.

His attraction to Anne disturbed him, caused him shame and guilt, but her absence had made it easier to conquer. He had achieved a degree of contentment knowing that she had gone on to a better, a more suitable life. He even took a certain comfort from her decision to return to Quebec, for she was safe and secure in the care of her uncle.

But now she was back.

34

After the children were in bed, and Liz and Anne had changed into nightgowns and robes, they were seated at the kitchen table, sipping the hot cocoa that Liz had just poured out.

"Hot," Anne commented, as she blew on the steaming liquid.

"Use a soup spoon," Liz suggested, and handed her one.

"My father would pour it in a saucer and slurp it."

"That's how my grandmother, back in Ireland, sipped her tea."

As if lost in memories, neither spoke for several minutes. The wick in the oil lamp in the middle of the table was turned low so that a circle of light illuminated only the tabletop. The two women rested in shadows.

"I don't believe I've ever known as peaceful an evening. It reminds me of the chapel at school. I used to slip in occasionally when it was empty. Just for the sense of peace I found there."

"I'm afraid I'm about to shatter this lovely calm. I need to ask you something." The older woman leaned across the table. "Do you think Ned would make a good husband?"

Anne grinned, "I've often wondered about you and Ned. He would make a perfectly marvelous husband. He is thoughtful, considerate. Wonderful with your children."

"No, no. Not me and Ned. You and Ned."

"Me?" Anne covered her face with her hands.

The older woman said nothing more. The clock over the sink ticked off the seconds.

"Your question frightens me, " Anne said, "and I don't know why."

She took a slight breath.

"I want to tell you about a man back in Quebec. His name is Paul. He gave me my first kiss, told me I was the loveliest woman he'd ever met. When Liam was unbearable, I used to pretend he was Paul, and it made things easier for me. When I returned to Quebec, I looked forward to seeing him again. He was such a disappointment. He was not even interesting."

"Can you say Ned is not interesting?"

"What I realized, after I met Paul again, is that I am a poor judge of men."

"Then what you said about Ned, that he's thoughtful, considerate, wonderful to my children, was untrue?"

Anne shook her head. "Of course he is all of those things. And much more. Has Ned said something to make you ask me such a question?"

"I'm just an old busybody, poking my nose where it doesn't belong. Let's get to bed. There's an extra blanket in the bottom dresser drawer if you need it."

The two women hugged good night.

In the small bedroom off the kitchen, where Ned formerly slept, Anne lay awake, for hours it seemed, reworking her conversation with Liz, trying to make all the pieces fit.

As she was about to slide into sleep, she saw again the wisp of curl that lay flat against Ned's nape and it made her smile.

35

The children's squeals brought Liz and Anne into the kitchen from the dining room. Ned was standing inside the back door, his arms filled with colorfully wrapped bundles. He had taken the early train up from Sparkill so they could all attend Christmas Mass together.

The children had already opened their gifts from under the tree. They fidgeted, anxious now to see what Ned had brought.

When Anne unwrapped the slender, square box, she was disappointed. Embroidered handkerchiefs. He had given Liz a beautiful pair of tan leather gloves. She rebuked herself. Ned probably didn't have spare money for gifts

"It will be a grand day for you to climb the Tor," Liz declared, as she passed the pancakes and sausages. "Tame these ruffians' high spirits," she chuckled, nodding across the table at the children.

She dismissed Anne's offers of help, assuring her that dinner was under way. "The turkey won't be cooked for hours. And, thanks to you, the table is set. So, get along, the lot of you."

The only sign of life in the otherwise deserted streets was an occasional horse-drawn carriage. Robbie and the two girls scampered ahead along Main Street, occasionally pausing at a shop to inspect its Christmas decorations.

"How well kept the stores are," Anne said. "It's hard to believe that less than a year ago everything was covered with soot and grime."

"People will never forget the landslide," Ned said. "But what's past is past."

When the children spotted the ice cream parlor on the other side of the street, Ned called out for them to wait so everyone could cross together.

Colorful Tiffany glass framed the top and sides of the half-bow windows of Lucas Confectionary. Large red-and-white candy canes were suspended above glass jars and bowls filled with lemon sticks, gumdrops, and chocolates. The children shielded their eyes as they peered into the darkened shop. Theresa explained to Anne that, on each child's birthday, they all sat around a square marble-topped table and their mother treated them to Lucas's home-made vanilla ice cream.

"Why does it have to be closed today?" Robbie pouted.

"So your mother won't kill me for ruining your appetite, " Ned teased.

"Mother never gets angry at you," Kate pointed out and Theresa nodded.

The afternoon was clear but windy and cold. From High Tor's summit, Anne looked down at her beloved Hudson.

"This is the finest tonic in the world," she said.

"It's a remarkable sight," Ned agreed.

Robbie ran over to where Ned and Anne sat on a rock. "Can we explore a bit and look for arrowheads? We won't go far," he promised.

Ned pulled a whistle from his pocket. "You three stay together and when you hear this whistle, you come running. Agreed?"

The little boy nodded and hurried off to his sisters, calling, "Ned says it's okay."

"Would you take a penny for your thoughts?" Ned asked gently.

Anne sighed. "So much has happened to me in one year."

She thought he had bent over to put the whistle back in his pocket, but saw him transfer it to his other hand. From the pocket, Ned drew out a tiny package. It was wrapped in gold paper and tied with a slim white ribbon.

With a tentative, expectant look, he handed it to her.

A cut glass bowl of cranberry sauce sat at one end of the table. At the other end, a footed glass held ribs of celery.

Everyone took their places for Ned to lead the blessing. Then the women and girls left to bring back a huge platter of sliced turkey, steaming bowls of mashed potatoes and turnip, and a brimming gravy boat.

Liz watched as the food was passed, pausing to catch her breath before helping herself. It was then that she caught sight of the ring.

She jumped up and ran to Anne. "Tell me! When did this happen?" She hugged her, and then hugged Ned.

"What?" Robbie asked. "What happened?"

Bewildered, the children watched as their mother pulled Ned and Anne from their chairs and circled them both in her arms. Hopping and stumbling, the adults roared with laughter. The little boy and his sisters ran and joined the dance, the feast forgotten.

Margaret Williams has earned a B.A. from St. John's University and an M.S.W. from Fordham University. She has worked as a social worker and planner for the elderly and has taught college classes in gerontology. She was awarded the Maxwell Anderson Prize for her short story, "Cat's Cradle." Margaret has four grown children and lives with her husband, Earl, in the Lower Hudson Valley.

Acknowledgements

While this is a work of fiction, in my pursuit of historical accuracy I have depended on numerous books, including *Within These Gates* by Daniel De Noyelles; *The Story of Brick* by Charles Elley Hall; *La Foi—La Langue—La Culture: The Franco-Americans of Biddeford, Maine* by Dr. Michael J. Guignard; *Immigrants From The North* by the Hyde School of Bath, Maine; *Nothing Is Quite Enough* by Dr. Gary MacEoin; and *Behind The Ballots: The Personal History of a Politician* by James A. Farley. Also, articles in *South of the Mountains*, *The Rockland County Journal*, *The Rockland County Times*, *The Nyack Evening Journal*, *The Nyack Evening Star*, and *The Journal News*.

Thanks to the personnel from these libraries in Rockland County: King's Daughters, Nyack, New City, Tompkins Cove, Finklestein, and Pearl River, as well as these in Maine: the McArthur Library in Biddeford, and the University of Southern Maine in Portland. Also the Historical Society of Rockland County, the Museum of the City of New York, the New York Historical Society, the Hudson River Maritime Museum, and the Biddeford Historical Society. I consulted the archives of the Haverstraw Brick Museum, Rockland County, The Dominican Sisters Convent of Sparkill, and St. Dominic's Home of Blauvelt.

I could not have written this book without the assistance of the board of the Haverstraw Brick Museum, particularly Jack Berrian, Thomas Sullivan, Patricia Gordon and Gail Lucas. Philip Rotella and Leonard Cooke graciously shared oral histories. Additional help came from Suzanne Belisle, John Belisle, Pauline Baiguy, Michael Guignard, Jack Pirkey, Charles Butler, Jeanne Gagne Emard, Charlene Paradis, and Dr. Maureen Smith.

GROW, my writing group—Melanie Kershaw, Cynthia Webb, and Neva Powell, under the indefatigable and unerring leadership of Renée Ashley—provided the soil and nourishment that brought this book to life.

My son, Christopher, my daughters, Martha, Jennifer, and Amanda, and above all, my patient and understanding husband, Earl, offered unwavering encouragement and love.

Recommended fine literary fiction from Avocet Press

The Long Crossing
Neva Powell

River Whispers
Glynn Marsh Alam

Resistance
and other short fiction
Christine Japely

Water Music
Melanie Kershaw